ROUTE 80

First Printing, 2025

ISBN paperback: 979-8-9923838-5-0
ISBN epub: 979-8-9923838-6-7

This book is dedicated to my beautiful wife, children, grandson, son in law, parents, sister, brother, nieces, nephews, family, friends who have become my extended family and to all who...

Never Say Surrender.

Thanks to my son for creating the title of this book.

The Road Not Taken

Two roads diverged in a yellow wood,
And sorry I could not travel both
And be one traveler, long I stood
And looked down one as far as I could
To where it bent in the undergrowth;
Then took the other, as just as fair,
And having perhaps the better claim,
Because it was grassy and wanted wear;
Though as for that the passing there
Had worn them really about the same,
And both that morning equally lay
In leaves no step had trodden black.
Oh, I kept the first for another day!
Yet knowing how way leads on to way,
I doubted if I should ever come back.
I shall be telling this with a sigh
Somewhere ages and ages hence:
Two roads diverged in a wood, and I—
I took the one less traveled by;
And that has made all the difference.
—Robert Frost, 1916

Route 80

Michael Conte

Raven + Grace
PRESS

Contents

1

Tug of War

A Picture-Perfect Wedding Day

I t's wedding day for my cousin Charlie and his bride, Maria. October 23, 1981. The reception is at the Twin Lakes Country Club on the North Fork of Long Island, New York.

The weather is unseasonably warm for autumn—seventy-one degrees and not a cloud in the sky. This time of year, the North Fork, with its fall foliage in fiery reds, oranges, and yellows, is postcard perfect. It's New York wine country, a tranquil retreat from city life, with vineyards stretching as far as the eye can see. For us New Yorkers, it's a sanctuary.

The Twin Lakes Country Club, nestled among these vineyards, boasts twenty-three acres of pristine property framed by twin lakes, vibrant trees, and ornate horse-drawn carriages. It's a magical place, the perfect setting for love and family unity.

But beneath this picturesque façade, an unforeseen event would soon unfold.

Italian Wedding Tradition

Italian weddings have their quirks, a mix of tradition and ego that can be almost comical.

Cash is the gift of choice—no blenders or toasters here, my friends. And the amount is rarely arbitrary; it's often calculated and based on what the giver received at their own wedding. For example, if the guest received X amount of money from the recipient family on their wedding day, then that *exact* amount would be gifted back when their children marry.

This is all previously calculated by a written log that is kept by every Italian newlywed couple. This ritual is then passed down from generation to generation. Some people even take it one step further where the amount of the gift could change at the reception depending on the quality of the food or the performance of the band. It's a dance of ego and bravado, and my family is no exception.

Welcome to the wonderful, chaotic world of being Italian.

A Life Pulled in Two Directions

At nineteen, I was living in Corona, Queens, with my mother, older brother, Dave, and younger sister, Grace.

My parents had recently divorced, and while the separation brought a sense of calm, it left behind a tension that lingered, ready to spark. My father's life was a volatile mix of charm and chaos—in and out of our lives, in and out of federal prison.

My mother, by contrast, was our steady anchor, our "moral advisor" holding the family together. My father's world had a magnetic pull. It was glamorous, wild, and intoxicating. His life choice, romanticized in movies and books, was as enticing as a beautiful woman or a dangerous drug. But it was also a path filled with turmoil and heartbreak.

I found myself constantly torn between these two worlds: my mother's path of stability and practicality, and my father's allure of intrigue and power.

It was a balancing act, a tightrope walk, and one without a safety net. I must admit, my father's path often stirs deep emotional stress and occasional anger within me, feelings I work hard to keep at bay, though I must confess, it's anything but easy.

The Wedding Ceremony

The wedding invitation read, "Holy Matrimony will commence promptly at 2:35 p.m. at Our Lady of Ostrabrama Roman Catholic

Church." I picked up my girlfriend, Antoinette, from her home in Bayside, Queens, and we headed east. The hour-and-fifteen-minute drive gave us time to catch up.

We were both students at Queens College—me in finance, her in computer science. She was always ahead of the pack; in 1981 computers were something out of a science-fiction TV show, and we all know where that technology wound up. I admired her intelligence, focus, and drive. My days were split between academia and nights working at my father's social club.

There, I managed card games, served drinks, and pocketed generous tips. The money was good, too good for a nineteen-year-old kid to resist. My life was a constant juggling act between the innocence of college life and the street-smart hustle of my father's world. Every day, I asked myself, *Where is all this leading?*

We arrived at the church at exactly 2:27 p.m. I quickly parked my Caddy just in time, as Maria pulled up in a white Rolls-Royce limousine, breathtaking in her gown. They say all brides are beautiful, but Maria was the epitome of beauty.

The ceremony was really moving, and as I sat beside Antoinette, holding her hand, I couldn't help but imagine our future together.

She was the one.

As the ceremony ended, the guests slowly filed out of the church, each taking their turn to congratulate the glowing bride and groom.

Soon after, our family gathered in front of the church for a celebratory photo, our smiles reflecting the joy of the occasion.

It was a truly happy moment, and we couldn't wait to head to the country club to continue the celebration and share in the love and happiness of this wonderful couple.

The drive to Twin Lakes was a quick ten minutes. My cousin Tina and her fiancé, Peter, hopped into my Caddy for the ride. Tina, a tough, no-nonsense gal from Queens, had big aspirations of being a "well-kept wife."

With pride in her voice, she announced, "Michael, Peter already knows that when we get married, he's putting me in the seat of a Cadillac Biarritz." (For all of you millennials, a Cadillac Biarritz was the Mercedes of its day).

I remember thinking, *I'm surrounded by lunatics.*

Then again, maybe I was a bit of a lunatic myself back then, chasing dreams, throwing caution to the wind, and hoping to snag a star along the way.

By the way, that's a good thing...

When we arrived at Twin Lakes, the valet service was manned by a group of twelve or so twenty-something, muscle-bound steroid freaks who looked like they spent more time at the gym than parking cars. I couldn't help but chuckle at the sight. The contrast between the elegance of the country club and these "mamalukes" struck me as jarring.

It was like pairing a three-thousand-dollar suit with white gym socks. But I shrugged off my judgmental thoughts, accepted the parking ticket, and headed inside.

After all, I was here to have the time of my life.

The Reception Begins

Once inside, the opulence of Twin Lakes was like something out of a high-end magazine. The space exuded Old English charm, with its plush drapes and light brown mahogany panels adorned with intricate carvings.

Every detail radiated sophistication and class.

Antoinette and I made our way to the cocktail hour room, where we found Dave with his girlfriend, Joanna, and Grace, with her other half, Nick, all sipping champagne.

The atmosphere was lively, and the food was nothing short of spectacular. Seven carving stations showcased a variety of meats and poultry, complemented by an extravagant seafood spread that included shrimp, lobster, crab, oysters, clams. Whatever you could dream of, they had it.

The entire family was there, and it was wonderful to see everyone together. This was what we call a "Top Shelf Affair."

After indulging in the cocktail hour, we moved to the grand ballroom for the reception. Words like "stunning" hardly did this room justice; it felt like stepping into Buckingham Palace itself.

We found our place cards and made our way to our assigned tables, ready to enjoy an unforgettable evening.

My Father's Crew

My father had his own table, surrounded by his friends better known as "his crew." It was an eclectic group of colorful characters, all men, no wives or girlfriends in sight. There was Fat Mike, a five-foot-nine, three-hundred-and-fifty-pound force of nature. Then there was Paulie the Torch, who chain-smoked three packs of cigarettes a day and was rarely seen without a lit one in hand. Tommy Guns—well, his nickname speaks for itself. Two-Footer was Marco, a five-foot-three bulldozer who got his name from his stocky, powerful build. Dougie Numbers ran a numbers racket in The Bronx, while Paulie Trees owned a Christmas tree farm and dabbled in a variety of other ventures. And finally, there was Johnny 9, who earned his moniker after losing a finger in a fight.

These men didn't fuck around. They were the kind of people you wouldn't want to fall out of favor with. But one thing about "street guys" is undeniable: they hold onto Old World Values. They're polite, courteous, and always willing to lend a hand to "friends of friends."

It's no surprise that neighborhoods where these guys live are often the safest places to be. Period! It's an unspoken code—they look out for one another and protect everyone in their community.

I have to admit, they're an easy group to like and respect, which is part of the appeal. That allure, however, often blurred my focus on the path my mother hoped for me to follow.

As we made our way to our assigned tables, a fourteen-piece band filled the air with the timeless Frank Sinatra tune, "Summer Wind."

The band had three lead singers: one for big band classics, one for rock and pop hits, and the third for disco and dance music.

The rock/pop singer was a black man with a small afro, and he wore a yarmulke, exuding charisma. He introduced the wedding party with flair, followed by the bride and groom, and the celebration officially kicked off.

The night was nothing short of magical, full of love, laughter, incredible food, and plenty of drinks.

We danced the night away, and at one point, family members even hopped onstage, borrowed the band's instruments, and put on an impromptu performance. After five unforgettable hours of fun and frolic, the evening came to an end. It was truly a wedding to remember, but little did we know, the real fun was just getting started...

The Parking Lot Brawl

As we made our way to the parking lot to retrieve our cars, I was with my father and his crew. I handed my valet ticket to one of the muscle-bound employees, as did my father and his friends. The wait dragged on far longer than expected, and these steroid-fueled guys had "a chip on their shoulder".

After about ten minutes, Johnny 9 finally had enough and snapped, "What the fuck is taking so long?"

One of the valets, clearly mistaking us for the usual Hamptons clientele, made the grave mistake of firing back, "Hey, who do you think you're talking to? Calm the fuck down!"

Well, let me tell you, that was a BIG FUCKING mistake. Just because these idiots had a few muscles, they thought that made them tough guys.

Well, they had no idea that they were looking down the barrel, eye to eye with REAL TOUGH GUYS. Before the word "down" even left the valet's mouth, Johnny 9 landed a punch so hard the kid nearly came out of his shoes.

My father stepped in, his voice booming with anger as he yelled at these punks. "You wanna be tough guys? We'll leave ya right where the fuck you're standing!"

In an instant, all the bravado drained from their faces.

They knew they'd messed with the wrong crowd. My father and his friends wasted no time, and the scene exploded into chaos. These so-called tough guys were getting the beating of a lifetime.

I don't know what came over me, but as I watched, something clicked. Without thinking, I jumped right into the middle of the brawl. It was twelve of them against nine of us, but numbers didn't matter. My father and his friends didn't just fight, they dominated.

They ripped rearview mirrors off cars and used them as weapons, swinging with precision. Keep in mind, these valets were in their mid-twenties, while my father and his crew were in their mid-to-late forties. But that didn't slow them down. When the mirrors weren't enough, they tore off the massive springs from the ornate horse carriages in the lot and began beating these guys with them. Cries for help echoed through the parking lot as blood splattered everywhere.

What had started as an elegant evening at a serene country club had turned into a full-blown war zone.

The Wake-Up Call

Within five minutes, the local police arrived, sirens wailing as a convoy of ten squad cars surrounded the scene. I tell ya, the once beautiful and peaceful club wasn't peaceful anymore. As we were taken away in cuffs, the so-called muscle-bound "tough guys" lay sprawled on the ground, battered and broken. As I sat in the back of the patrol car, waves of anger and regret washed over me. I kept asking myself, *What the fuck did I just do? Why did I let myself get pulled into this? I could be arrested—maybe even go to jail. What was I thinking?*

I knew better. Deep down, I knew this way of life wasn't for me. But resisting its pull wasn't always easy. The nerves hit me hard. My mind spiraled. *If I end up with a felony or a criminal record, I can kiss my hopes of a career in finance goodbye. I have goals. I'm in college. Antoinette won't want to build a life with someone who can't match her ambition or vision. What the fuck have I done?*

We were held in the local jail for about two hours. My father and his crew couldn't have cared less. They sat there laughing and joking like it was just another night. But I was sick to my stomach, sitting quietly with my thoughts. All I could think about was my mother and how deeply disappointed she would be. I felt like I had let her down. I knew this wasn't the road I wanted to be on; it was never my path. But living in a world surrounded by these influences made it hard to stay steady.

I realized then and there that I needed to chart my own course, one that aligned with my dreams and values, not the expectations or behaviors of those around me. I sat there, silently praying for a way out of this mess. And somehow, God must have been watching over me.

The twelve valets decided not to press charges. Maybe they didn't want to risk future problems, or maybe the owners of Twin Lakes, who were friends of ours, intervened. I don't know for sure. But I caught a break, and it felt like a second chance—a lifeline.

Relief swept over me but so did anger.

Not directly at my father, but at the chaos his life seemed to invite. His world complicated everything, creating confusion and anxiety that often felt overwhelming. My life was different from most, and I knew I had to find the courage to stand firm in my convictions.

This was my moment to stop playing tug-of-war with my emotions and start finding my own balance, my own path. Sitting in that cell, I made a vow to myself. I had to choose a path—not my father's, not the one that tempted me with easy money and fleeting power.

I had to find my own way, one that aligned with the life I wanted with Antoinette and the future I dreamed of.

I was going to have to be courageous, stand strong with my convictions and combat my emotional balancing act and see my way through this Tug of War.

2

The Call

The Call That Changed Everything

It was exactly 10:17 on a Tuesday morning, June 3, 2023, when the phone in my office rang.

A typical day in the heart of New York City, sun shining bright, the hum of ambition and energy pulsing through the streets below. My office sat just across from the New York Stock Exchange, five blocks from the World Trade Center.

After years of relentless work, I had built the life I once feared I had thrown away. I was here. A financial advisor, respected, successful. A man with a future.

My assistant's voice crackled through the intercom, breaking my moment of reflection. "You need to take this call. It's important."

I picked up the phone, expecting another client or maybe a colleague with last-minute market news.

Instead, the voice on the other end sent a chill down my spine. "Mr. Conte, this is Warden Dean Scurti from Lewisburg Federal Penitentiary."

In an instant, my world shifted.

My heart stopped.

Fuck.

Not this again.

My father had been incarcerated there for the past ten years, the latest chapter in a lifetime spent skirting the edges of the law. No matter how much distance I had put between us, his life still had the power to reach into mine and pull me back into its chaos.

"We need to verify Next of Kin records. Can you confirm your name and relationship?"

I hesitated, then answered, my voice even but laced with unease. "Yes. I'm his son."

There was no pause, no softening of words. Just a blunt statement that cracked through the line like a gunshot. "Your father was found dead in his cell early this morning."

I didn't move. Didn't blink. It felt like a bad joke, some cruel prank designed to shake me. But then the warden read off my father's Federal ID number—numbers I knew by heart, etched into my memory from decades of court dates, visiting rooms, and collect calls. It was real. I gripped the phone, my knuckles turning white, but I didn't say a word.

What was there to say?

Scurti gave me the standard protocol: how to claim the body, which funeral directors handled prison deaths, the cold logistics of closing a life like it was just another bureaucratic task.

Then he hung up. That was it. No sympathy. No time to process. Just information delivered without emotion.

That's how it was in the system. Inmates didn't get the benefit of sorrow or ceremony. They died as they lived, file numbers in a system that didn't give a damn.

I placed the receiver down gently, my hands suddenly feeling foreign, detached from my body.

I stared at the wall in front of me, but I wasn't in my office anymore. I was somewhere else. Someone else. Memories flooded in—his laughter during a card game at his social club, the smell of his strong cologne, his perfectly manicured fingernails, and his diamond pendant with the number thirteen. The good and the bad, tangled together in a life lived unapologetically. I never condoned his choices, but I never judged him either. That was the contradiction that had always lived inside me.

I had spent my life walking a fine line, trying to carve out my own path while carrying the weight of his legacy. And now, just like that, it was over. I should have felt relief. But all I felt was an emptiness I didn't know how to name.

The world outside my office kept moving, stocks rose and fell, people shouted on trading floors, life pulsed on without pause.

But inside, my world had stopped. For the first time in years, I felt like that kid sitting in the back of the patrol car again, caught between two lives. And I had no idea which one would claim me now. As I sat there thinking, my mind spun in a million directions while I prepared to call my siblings.

The Middle Child

I have a brother and sister, then there's me, the middle child. Some so-called experts talk about 'middle child syndrome,' whatever the hell that means.

I never felt it. In fact, I loved being in the middle. When we were kids, I used to joke with my brother and sister that when God created the oldest, he was taking his first shot at perfection but made a few mistakes. Then, with the second child, he corrected those errors thus, perfection was achieved.

By the third, even God couldn't make lightning strike twice, so he just fell a little short again. That's why the middle child was, let's just say...special.

My brother and sister would roll their eyes and just say, "Fuck you!" I played it off as a joke, but deep down, I kind of believed it.

I needed to call them both at once, so I dialed David first.

Similar to me, he had wrestled with the same temptations, but now he was a partner in a successful construction company in the city. I told him to hold while I called our sister, Grace, who owned a thriving hair and spa salon.

Luck was on my side, I caught her between clients. Breaking the news was harder than I expected. They were both silent at first, absorbing the weight of it. Then, like me, their thoughts shifted from grief to logistics. What was next? What were the protocols? That was our way. We were tough as nails, raised on hardship, conditioned to survive. That didn't mean we were cold, it just meant we knew how to keep it moving.

I knew they would grieve in their own way later, in their own time. For now, we just handled it, because as a family, we all lived by the attitude, "It is what it is."

Before hanging up, David said he would call our mother to break the news.

A Complicated Love Story

My parents had a complicated history. Married in 1959, high school sweethearts, they had weathered countless storms before finally divorcing. My mother had moved on, remarried, but I always wondered, *Do you ever truly move on from a love like that?* She had known my father since they were fourteen.

They had history, a bond no one else could fully understand. When I was younger, I took pride in that. I liked knowing they had teenage memories together, like something out of a movie. Maybe that's why my sister and I both ended up with long-term partners from our youth.

People say it takes two to tango, but to me, my father was just too young and not ready for marriage. I mean who would be at twenty-two years old? I know I wasn't.

Welcome to the Family

We were raised by parents from two completely different worlds. My mother's family was hard-working blue-collar immigrants striving for a better future. My grandfather, Dominic, arrived in America from Italy at five years old. By day, he worked as a plumber in the union, and by night, he studied relentlessly to earn his college degree. My grandmother Lena worked multiple jobs to help keep their modest household afloat. My mom grew up poor in Long Island City, Queens, in an old house with dirt floors, sharing space with her parents and grandparents. Tragedy struck when a fire, started by a young cousin playing with matches, engulfed their home, killing both her grandparents and her three-year-old cousin.

My mother rarely spoke about it, some wounds were buried too deep. But in time, her father helped organize the plumbers' union in New York City, securing work for friends and family, including my father, though he never had the passion for it. He would go on to seek fortune and adventure elsewhere (we'll get to that later).

My father's family, on the other hand, was vastly different. His grandparents immigrated to America in the early 1900s, chasing the same dream of opportunity that drew so many others.

My grandparents were both born in the Lower East Side of New York City, a rough and bustling neighborhood where survival required more than just hard work...it demanded street smarts.

My grandmother Josie's family held onto that immigrant work ethic, embracing an honest living and doing whatever it took to make ends meet. But my grandfather and his brothers chose a different path.

Growing up in a predominantly Italian neighborhood, they were surrounded by a very different kind of influence. There was a "secret Italian organization" that ruled those streets. They were both feared and revered, the ultimate role models for young men looking for power, respect, and fast money. My grandfather had three brothers and a sister.

Only one brother and the sister stayed clear of any "questionable" activity. The brother who walked the straight path became a postman, living a quiet, respectable life. The others? Not so much. One of them, John, served a life sentence and ultimately died in prison. No one ever spoke of why. Another, Butch, was a notorious street enforcer who once shot a cop. The only reason the officer survived was pure luck; the bullet hit his badge instead of his heart. Crazy, huh?

Then there was my grandfather, Vinny Diamond. A bookmaker with ties to some of the biggest "names" of his time, he earned his nickname because he always wore flashy diamonds and drove nothing but Cadillacs. He looked the part of a movie gangster, and in many ways, he lived it. He ran his bookmaking operation out of Belmont and Aqueduct racetracks, the perfect hunting ground for gamblers desperate to place a bet. It was simple: If you wanted to take action, you had to be where the action was.

It reminds me of the old line from bank robber Willie Sutton. When asked why he robbed banks, he answered, "Because that's where the money is." The same logic applied to my grandfather. If you were going to run a book, you planted yourself among the people who couldn't resist the thrill of the gamble.

Makes sense, no?

Growing up, I'd hear wild stories from my grandfather about his days "in the life"...some shocking, some hilarious, all unbelievable.

One that stuck with me was the time he was driving through Harlem on his way to Yankee Stadium with his crew. A man stepped in front of his car, slowing them down. His friend in the passenger seat, impatient and eager to get to the game, barked, "Vinny, run this cocksucker down!"

So, without hesitation, my grandfather did just that. Left the guy in the street...I sat there, wide-eyed, unable to process what I had just heard.

As I got older and found myself in my own crazy situations, I often thought back to those stories and shook my head.

You can't make this shit up.

Every winter, my grandfather and his crew would escape New York's brutal cold and head to Miami for three months. They were all married, but the wives stayed back to raise the kids while the men went south to "conduct business" and enjoy the sunshine.

No one questioned it. That was just how things were done. Not sure how that arrangement would fly today...

I mentioned earlier that my mother was an only child, but my dad had a brother. His name was Paul, but to everyone outside the family, he was Rich or Richie. The name change wasn't just for fun, he had dreams of being a big band singer, like Frank Sinatra or Tony Bennett.

His stage name? Richie Martino.

To us, though, he was always Uncle Richie. He was a character, to say the least, not exactly a good guy, and he never worked a legitimate day in his life. He was destined for one of two careers: music or crime. Since the music career never took off, well, you can guess which path he chose.

When I was a kid, family weddings were like live concerts. When the band took a break, it was showtime. My father's Uncle Vincie would get on the drums, Cousin John would pick up the guitar, Cousin Albert would play sax, and Uncle Richie would take center stage and sing.

It was mesmerizing, like something out of a movie. This family had a personality—big, loud, unforgettable. I have to admit, I was drawn to my grandfather's world. It was flashy, it exuded power, and to a kid, it looked like the kind of life worth chasing.

My grandfather, Vinny, who I called Diamond and he loved it, owned a record store in Lower Manhattan, right on Bowery and Delancey. It wasn't just a place to buy music; it was an institution.

He carried both Spanish and American records, and the walls were lined with Spanish guitars for sale. As a kid, I thought it was amazing that Diamond was into music. Only later did I find out that the store had a backroom operation where he was "banging out" fugazzi credit cards.

So much for the arts! I loved Diamond though, he was larger than life and he had a nickname that was right out of a Hollywood movie. None of my friends had a grandfather called Diamond. I mean, really, what's not to like? That alone set me apart.

I knew from an early age that my family wasn't like everyone else's. And honestly? I loved it. It was thrilling. I was all in.

His record store was in a rough neighborhood, full of people looking to rob and steal. But Diamond's store? Untouchable. Everyone knew better than to mess with it. Why? Well, that came down to one legendary story I heard as a teenager.

One day, my father, Uncle Richie, and Diamond caught a guy stealing records. They didn't call the cops. That wasn't how things worked. Instead, they took him outside, held him down, and Diamond ran over his hands with his Cadillac.

Needless to say, no one ever tried to steal from that store again. At times there is nothing better than street justice. They would never call a cop; they policed themselves and they got much better results. A popular family tradition was that every car had a Sicilian horn, a long red pepper-shaped charm, hanging from the rearview mirror, with a Louisville Slugger resting on the floor in the back.

As soon as we started driving, this was the street protocol we followed. Hey, what's wrong with passing down traditions to the next generation? That's what families do. My father had a way of offering advice that was...unique.

When I was about eight years old, he pulled me aside and said, with complete seriousness, "Michael, if you ever get into a fight with someone bigger than you, just crack him over the head with a fucking baseball bat."

I remember staring at him, thinking, *Really? Were my friends' fathers giving them the same kind of wisdom?*

Growing up surrounded by this environment was intoxicating, exciting, even. It was easy to see how someone could be pulled into it, how the energy, the rules, the power could shape you.

My Greatest Influence

My mother? SHE WASN'T HAVING IT. Every single day, she fought for our souls. She wasn't about to let us be swallowed by that world, and she never backed down. That lifestyle wasn't for her, and she was willing to fight against the tide every step of the way.

My mother's name is Millie, but everyone calls her Chickie. Why? I never really knew. With that generation, things were what they were, no explanations necessary.

They didn't elaborate on things the way people do today. Now, today's generation? Well, that's another story.

When my mom was young, she was beautiful and incredibly smart. She was part of an accelerated program in high school, graduating a year ahead of her class.

She was encouraged to go to college, but back in the 1950s, that wasn't the typical path for young women. Instead, like so many others in her peer group, she graduated high school, got married, and settled into family life.

By twenty-two, she was married. By twenty-three, she had her first child. By twenty-four, her second.

Can you imagine this generation having two kids by the age of twenty-four? It must have felt stifling, suppressing—never getting the chance to fully explore the world, to chase new experiences, to realize their full potential.

For the generations that followed, the possibilities seemed endless. Society had opened up, offering new paths and perspectives. But for my mother's generation, expectations were set in stone. She eventually took an office job in Manhattan, but that ended the moment she got married. Her life became her husband and her children, and she gave herself to that role completely.

She was an only child, and years later, she would tell me how lonely that had been.

Looking back, I can see how much she poured herself into us, maybe because she had spent so much of her own childhood without the kind of companionship siblings bring. She may not have had choices, but she made damn sure we would. Her parents had a strained marriage and largely kept to themselves. She was deeply close to her father, admiring his intelligence and fiercely independent spirit—traits I believe she inherited. He was her benchmark, shaping her moral compass and instilling in her an unwavering sense of righteousness.

My mother embraced those principle values as her own. Her relationship with her mother, however, was distant. I remember my grandmother as cold and somewhat joyless, never the warm, inviting type, though she shared a special bond with my sister Grace. Looking back, I realize she may have carried burdens we never understood. As an adult, I can offer her the grace of perspective, though as a child, I simply saw her as unkind.

My grandfather, on the other hand, left a lasting impression. He was a straight-shooting, no-nonsense man who commanded respect. He passed away from leukemia when I was ten, so I never got to know him deeply, but I do know he profoundly shaped my mother. I'll never forget the day he died when my mother locked herself in her room, sobbing. Even now, that sound outside her bedroom door stays with me. There was a song that was popular then, "Alone Again (Naturally)" by Gilbert O'Sullivan. It was a favorite of my mothers.

Decades later, whenever I hear it, I'm transported back to that day, to that overwhelming grief. Life's trajectory can change in an instant, reshaping everything we thought we knew. As I've grown older, I've learned to embrace the unpredictability of life and to live in the present. There's an old proverb that rings true: "If you're depressed, you're living in the past. If you're anxious, you're living in the future. If you're content, you're living in the present."

I often wonder how different life might have been if he had lived longer, if some of the chaos that followed could have been tempered by his presence. But I've learned not to dwell on the "what ifs." They only drain energy and lead nowhere. When my parents separated, we moved from Astoria, Queens, to Lindenhurst, Long Island, for about a year, living with my mother's parents. To me, it felt like moving to the "country". The sound of birds chirping was foreign, almost unsettling.

Queens

After my parents reconciled and my sister was born we moved again, this time to Jackson Heights, Queens, to live with my father's parents. That house was an adventure all its own—full of drama, yelling, and chaos. Classic Italian, right? Well maybe not...

My grandparents' relationship was volatile, my mother later telling me much of it stemmed from Diamond's wandering eye. Let's say he liked to shake it up a little bit. Capisce?

But despite all the noise, one thing was certain: Diamond never raised his hands to a woman. That wasn't his way.

That said, I do remember the time my grandmother sliced him under his nose with a paring knife, right above his upper lip. It happened right in front of me! They made up soon after, and for some reason, I wasn't traumatized or scared. I must have been around seven, and my only thought was, *Well, that's crazy.* And then I moved on.

Jackson Heights in the 1960s was a tough, blue-collar neighborhood, filled with Italian, Irish, and German families. You had to know how to fight. There was no getting around it. I started school there and was placed directly in first grade, skipping kindergarten. It wasn't because I was a genius; it had to do with birthdates and the school cutoff between Queens and Long Island.

Because I missed kindergarten, I was behind academically. My mother realized this immediately and took it upon herself to ensure I caught up. Every night, she worked with me, making sure my homework was done. Failure wasn't an option. Back then, classes were ranked from highest to lowest such as 2-1 being the smartest, 2-5 the lowest.

I hovered in the middle, always around the 1-4 or 2-3 range. Back then, you were reminded of your place every single day. Times have changed. Now, every kid gets a participation trophy. I think that's bullshit. There's nothing wrong with knowing where you stand, facing challenges head-on, and pushing yourself to be better. Hard work builds character and confidence.

If you're lucky, you'll meet people along the way who change your life. I was lucky. In third grade, my class was completely unruly, bordering on uncontrollable. We treated school like recess. I wasn't a troublemaker, never a bully, but I was hyper and easily distracted. My mother worked with me every night, but I would get frustrated, yelling, "MA, LISTEN TO ME!"

I wasn't exactly calm, cool, or collected.

She would just say, "Michael, count to ten and calm down." I can still hear her voice saying it today.

At one point, a doctor suggested putting me on calming medication. My mother tried it once, saw the difference, and immediately stopped. "I'll just deal with it," she said.

She chose to manage my wild energy with patience and discipline rather than medication. She believed in me, even when I didn't believe in myself.

Mrs. Rosa

Then came Mrs. Rosa Payne. She was a retired teacher, the first African American female teacher in the NYC school system. She had left teaching, but the school brought her back specifically to handle my out-of-control third-grade class. And she did. From the first day, she was a disciplinarian, in complete sync with my mother. Like my mom, Mrs. Payne believed in education, good behavior, and self-respect. My mother loved her because, for the first time, she had an ally. At parent-teacher conferences (which my mother NEVER missed), Mrs. Payne would say, "I've got him during the day, you've got him at night."

They both believed I was like a piece of coal—apply enough pressure, and I'd turn into a diamond. And you know what? I like to believe that's exactly what happened.

I was relieved when third grade ended, thinking I'd finally get an easier teacher. But Mrs. Payne stayed another year, following my class into fourth grade. She wasn't done molding me yet, and my mother was thrilled. If you're lucky, life gives you angels. Mrs. Payne was one of mine.

Life is full of tipping points, moments where you either rise or fall. When you pay attention, you can recognize them and respond accordingly. My mother and Mrs. Payne made me who I am.

Today, with my own children, I have pushed them the way they pushed me. Not because I want to control them, but because I want them to be their best.

Oh, and Mrs. Payne? Years later, she was honored in a big way. The city renamed P.S. 637 to the P.S. 637 Rosa Payne School. Pretty cool, huh?

If you're wondering, I'll talk more about my father as the story unfolds. This isn't about bashing him—far from it. His way of life shaped me too, and I loved and respected him for who he was. He always told me, "It's good to be book smart, but without street smarts, you're nothing." And he was right.

So I got two educations—one from the classroom and one from "the street". His world was chaotic, and at times, it pulled at me. But looking back, I see how it made me more reflective, more self-aware. As crazy as it sounds, I wouldn't have wanted a different journey. It shaped me, taught me, and ultimately solidified what I truly wanted from life. There's an old saying: "If life gives you lemons, make lemonade." I like to think that's exactly what I did. Thanks, Dad. Love you. Miss you.

Now the journey begins after The Call.

3

Road Trip

Wednesday morning. The day after receiving *the call* from Warden Scurti. Another road trip.

I probably got three hours of sleep, tossing and turning, my mind tangled in nervous energy and apprehension over what lies ahead. Over the years, these road trips have become routine. Unfortunately. Not the kind of trip that leads to Disney™ or some long-awaited vacation. No, these were different.

My father was in and out of federal prisons. The weight of that is hard to explain to someone who hasn't lived it. It's a roller coaster, one you don't choose to ride but have to endure. You learn to adapt, survive, and accept the situation because there's no other choice. That's why our family is made up of survivors.

After a while, you grow numb to the unpredictable twists and turns of life. The only option is to say, "It is what it is," switch into *combat mode*, and push forward. In time, I became tougher than the rest.

Yet, these so-called road trips weren't always just about duty or obligation. Sometimes, they were filled with unexpected moments of humor and warmth. And always, they gave me space for introspection. If I had middle names, they'd be 'introspective and reflective'.

Like most people, I spent my formative years weighing career choices, contemplating what kind of life I wanted. The only difference? Choosing wrong in my world had much harsher consequences. It was a constant psychological exercise, balancing the lure of glitz and glamour against the slow and steady path. Navigating the conflicting philosophies of my parents while holding onto my own principles. Easier said than done. But I was always a work in progress.

This particular Wednesday was a typical June day in New York with plenty of sunshine, the warm seasonal air ushering in the start of summer. There's nothing like the beginning of summer, leaving behind another dreary, depressing winter. It's a season of hope.

So, we packed up the car and headed out for the long ride to Pennsylvania. These road trips were our version of seeing the country since vacations were never a thing in our family. Over the years, we had made stops in Pennsylvania, Kentucky, Georgia,

South Jersey, Connecticut, and North Carolina. Along the way, we'd pull over to eat, use the restroom, or just take a break from the hours of driving. We usually traveled in a small group, three or four of us at a time. Always family, sometimes friends, who often became the most interesting part of the journey. Some of them I'd known for years; others were former inmates of my father's. Occasionally, I would meet these guys *on* the day of the trip. Interesting, but we'll get to that later.

Long trips have a way of revealing people. The extended hours on the road strip away the distractions of daily life. It's a relaxed setting—no rush, no interruptions—and you find yourself engaged in conversations that might never happen otherwise. In that car, people let their guard down. They talk. And you learn who they really are.

But this trip felt different. It carried a heavier weight, a sense of finality. Reflection hung in the air like an unspoken agreement between us.

On this last journey, I traveled with Dave and my cousin, Anthony—though we just called him Cousin. He was from my father's side, born and raised in Queens, just like us. There's something about people from Queens. We're all cut from the same cloth, straight shooters, no bullshit, with a little bit of a chip on our shoulders. We grew up in schoolyards, not malls. No play dates, no hand-holding through life. Summers were spent on school yards, navigating a mix of personalities and learning how to thrive on wits alone. It was the best education you could get.

Even as an adult, after moving to Long Island, that Queens identity never left me. Whenever someone asks where I'm from, my answer is always the same. "My home is Long Island, but my heart is Queens. I COME FROM QUEENS!" That's the chip I'm talking about.

Traveling with Cousin was like a blast from the past for my brother and me. Through countless trials and tribulations, Dave and I successfully steered away from the life my father had so proudly chosen. But for Cousin, that road was a badge of honor. When we were younger, he was running a bookmaking business, making what seemed like 'easy money'.

Though our paths diverged, we always stayed in touch—at arm's length. That is, until he got pinched and did two years in Danbury Penitentiary. There was always love and mutual respect, but different roads lead to different destinations. He was in the fast lane, while, thanks to our mother's guidance, my brother and I chose the middle.

Each of these road trips had their own character, their own energy. Some were filled with playful banter and jokes, just guys fucking around. But this one? This one was all about "remember when?" The conversation shifted from laughter to deep emotion, from jokes to the bittersweet ache of time lost. Sound familiar? We've all had those moments. Where did the time go?

The real trick I've learned is not just looking back but realizing the value of the present. Grabbing onto it with both hands and not letting go.

We left for our trip from Corona, Queens, just after sunrise at 6:13 a.m. The journey, with stops, would take about five hours. After my grandfather Dominic passed, my mom inherited some money, and our family moved from Astoria to Jackson Heights when I was ten. Back then, my father was still a union plumber. His *real* life choices were still a few years ahead. If only he had a crystal ball, maybe things would have been easier, maybe they'd have been different. I wonder if he ever regretted his choice.

Sad thing is, even if he did, he'd never admit it.

But if I had to guess?

He did.

A Look Back...

September 1972. We moved into our new home in Corona the night before the school year started. Imagine waking up in a new neighborhood, not knowing a single soul, and having to start at a new school the very next day. It felt like landing on Mars, completely foreign and unsettling. To say I was nervous would be an understatement.

But within a week, I had new friends, and I was off and running. I was entering sixth grade at P.S. 215, while my sister started first grade. My new teacher was an interesting lady. What is it with me and these teachers? Her name was Ms. Gold, but she insisted we call her by her first name, Doris. So, Doris it was.

Doris was a short, stocky woman with spiky hair and a spunky attitude. She drove a Volkswagen bus, the kind that was all the rage in the late '60s and early '70s. She was different from any teacher I'd ever had. First, she wanted to be called by her first name. Second, she was a Ms. not a Mrs., and third she lived alone with her cats. As an adult, I now realize she was a lesbian. Back then, we sensed something was different, but it didn't matter. We never cared. She was an incredible teacher who believed in me and pushed me to be better.

She appointed me Captain of the Safety Patrol—something I didn't necessarily want, but she gave me no choice. My job was to oversee the sixth-grade crossing guards, and I got to pick my best friend as my lieutenant. I even got a shoulder belt with a big badge that read *CAPTAIN*. I thought it was a little dorky, but I didn't want to let Doris down.

Every year, each class put on a play. Most teachers chose a Broadway show and had the students perform it. Not Doris. She wrote her own script, composed original music, and it was about an all-American boy whose younger brother was disabled. Guess who played the all-American boy?

Yep. Yours truly.

The play was a hit, and we were even asked to perform it at other schools, including the junior high I would attend the following year. Some scenes were tough for a sixth grader. I had to kiss a girl on the cheek, who played my mother, and I had to cry when my brother died.

Doris also taught me the value of stepping outside my comfort zone. That lesson stuck with me. Years later, as a young financial advisor, I had to cold call potential clients—complete strangers—to pitch them stocks. It was nerve-wracking and uncomfortable, just like that stage performance.

Many of my colleagues quit within two months.

Today, I'm in my thirty-first year in finance.

I guess Doris was preparing me for success all along.

Thanks, Doris!

Back to the neighborhood of Corona, one of the greatest places to grow up. More suburban than Jackson Heights, it was predominantly Italian with a small Greek presence. It was the kind of neighborhood where everyone had a family member "affiliated" in some way. There was always that classic line, "Do you know who my uncle is?" That kind of bullshit.

All my closest friends on the block were Italian: Nino, Swaggy, Sal, Duck, my brother, and me. We were a tight-knit crew of six. We lived right across the street from the junior high school where my siblings and I went. Despite the convenience, I was late to school most days, which drove my mother crazy.

Our real home wasn't inside our houses—it was the schoolyard, which we called The Park. With small backyards and no pools, our lives revolved around that space. We played sports all day, and by the time we hit twelve or thirteen, we were drinking beer and hooking up with neighborhood girls. Life came at me fast, and I grabbed onto it with both hands.

The Park was where everything happened. Like I said...Corona was the perfect place to grow up.

Back on the Road

As we began our journey south to Lewisburg, Pennsylvania, the sun was just beginning to rise, casting its reflection on the Whitestone Bridge. It was a breathtaking sight. Whitestone Bridge sits along the East River, offering views that can be truly majestic.

I took the first shift driving, with my brother riding shotgun and Cousin in the backseat. Grace stayed behind to take care of my mother, who had been struggling with health issues. We were in my SUV, headed to identify my father's body and to make arrangements with the funeral home. Just saying those words brought back a deep unease. This wasn't like any of our other road trips.

As we crossed the bridge and entered the Bronx, the conversation turned to my father. We reminisced, reflected, and we enjoyed shooting the breeze, as we always did.

Then, out of nowhere, Cousin—who idolized my father—blurted, "Hey, remember when your father saved Junior from choking?"

A chill ran down my spine. "REMEMBER?!" I shouted. "I was there!"

Three Whacks

My parents kept a small crystal bowl filled with Life Savers™ candies on the living room table. One day, my younger cousin Junior's family came over before heading to a men's softball game; his father, Uncle Nick, played in the league. I was eleven at the time, and they had stopped by to pick me up and take me to watch the game.

Suddenly, Junior came into the kitchen from the living room, choking and gasping for air. He had put a candy in his mouth, and it got lodged in his throat. I froze. I had no idea what to do. It escalated fast. Junior started turning blue. Uncle Nick, in a panic, was jamming his fingers down Junior's throat, desperately trying to clear the obstruction, but nothing was working. Blood started pouring from his mouth. I stood there, horrified, convinced we were about to watch him die right in front of us.

Then, suddenly, my father took charge. Without hesitation, he grabbed Junior by the ankles, turned him upside down, and hit him hard between the shoulder blades. One. Two. Three solid whacks, and that candy popped right out.

Cousin's eyes went wide. "Shit! I didn't know you were there! That's crazy!"

To this day, Junior owes his life to my father. That moment, as terrifying as it was, proved what I had always known—my father was built for situations like that.

There's this show on TV where the host interviews celebrities in an hour-long Q&A about their lives. At the end, the host always asks, "If you were in a foxhole, who would you want in there with you to get you out?"

For me, that answer is easy. My father. One hundred percent. Because I know for damn sure that I'm getting out alive.

The Cost of Loyalty

My father was not a great husband, but I'll tell you what, he was loyal. He was a man's man, a friend you were lucky to have. Always respectful, always courteous. But don't mistake kindness for weakness—that would be a bad idea.

Like I said earlier, my father started dating my mom when he was fourteen. He was the younger of two brothers and had a goodness about him. Unlike his brother and Diamond, who were destined for the streets, my father stayed responsible. He quit high school after tenth grade, not because he was reckless, but because school wasn't for him. Instead, he took on jobs, working hard to support himself.

My mother would tell me later that even when they were teenagers, it was obvious his parents favored his older brother. They coddled him, treated him like he could do no wrong. She felt bad for my father and would bring it up to him, but he never acknowledged it. Maybe he felt that slight, but he wouldn't admit it. He was loyal to his family, to his brother, no matter how undeserving.

That loyalty cost him. My uncle constantly screwed up, dragging my father into bad situations. My father spent a lot of money fixing problems his brother created, but that prick didn't care. He was a narcissist who couldn't even spell the word *loyalty*, let alone live by it.

Take their weddings, for example. When my father got married, he chose his brother as his best man. A year later, when my uncle got married, he picked some random friend instead. That's just how it was. The cycle repeated itself over and over. My father never wavered, never walked away. Maybe he didn't want to disappoint his parents. Maybe he felt obligated as the responsible one. I don't know. Even now, I don't have the answer.

No matter how much my uncle took advantage, my father forgave him, pulling him into business ventures that always ended in disaster. My father had his faults, like us all, but his loyalty—his unwavering commitment to people and his convictions—was something to admire.

When my father turned eighteen, he and his friends enlisted in the United States Army to fight in the Korean War. Years later, I asked him, "Why enlist? Why not wait to see if you'd get drafted?"

He shrugged. "It was inevitable, so we figured we'd just get it over with."

He was shipped to Fort Bragg in North Carolina, where he *volunteered* to parachute out of planes for five dollars a day. Every cent went straight home to his parents for savings. Let me tell you, no amount of money could get me to jump out of a plane. Five thousand a day? Not happening.

After basic training, he was sent straight to the front lines in Korea. My uncle? When he was drafted, my grandfather made sure he enlisted as an entertainer. He never saw combat. Skated right through.

When my father came back, he married my mom immediately. But he wasn't the same. He had these blood-curdling nightmares that shook the walls of the house. As kids, we never knew when we'd be jolted awake by his screams. Today, they'd call it Post Traumatic Stress Disorder (PTSD). Back then, it was just something we lived with.

Decades later, he told me something that shook me to my core. Out of four hundred men, he and another soldier had been chosen to stay at Fort Bragg to learn new combat tank technology. They didn't *have* to go to Korea.

I asked, "Then why the hell did you go?"

He looked me in the eye and said, "I wanted to stay with my friends."

Even after all the nightmares, after all the trauma, he had *chosen* to go to war.

Loyalty.

It's the most important trait I learned from him. It's in my DNA. My close friends know it and appreciate it. And for those who aren't cut from the same cloth? I move off them.

Guys like me and my father? We don't grow on trees.

On the Road Again

I had been driving for about an hour and a half when we decided to make our first stop for breakfast. It was early June, and the heat and humidity reminded us that spring was officially in the rearview mirror.

Stopping off in small towns always felt surreal, like stepping onto another planet. We were kids from Queens—we all talked the same and cursed like bandits. Seeing how people lived outside our world was always an amusing experience. The waitresses at these roadside diners loved our accents.

They'd say, "Talk some more, I love your accent."

And we'd laugh, "Really? We think *you* have the accent." That chip on the shoulder is always there.

We pulled into a small town called Franklin Lakes and found a diner, Franklin Diner. It had a cozy, nostalgic feel, like stepping back into the 1960s. Jukeboxes sat on each table, fifty cents a song. We picked Bobby Darin's "Mack the Knife"—a classic.

Our waitress, Kathy, was a middle-aged woman with short blonde hair and striking blue-green eyes. She took our orders, and as we waited for our food, I started talking about past road trips with Diamond and all the fucking craziness.

Cousin loved Diamond. He was always excited to hear another story.

"Cousin, let me tell you. When we traveled with Diamond, the car rides were usually quiet, but the moment we stopped for food? All bets were off."

I continued. "We were loud, I mean really LOUD. And when it came time to order, Diamond would always say, 'Mikey, whatever you want, I got it.' I'd tell him, 'Diamond, really not necessary, no worries.' And he'd bark back, 'I'd like to step on your head and watch your eyeballs pop out, just order the food!'"

Cousin burst out laughing.

"On some of these trips, we had two cars packed with family and friends," I explained. "That's why I'd say it wasn't necessary. There were like eight of us. But he wouldn't hear it. We'd order big. Omelets, burgers, fries. The table was *covered* in food."

"Oh, and I forgot to mention? Diamond had this insane cough. Sounded like he had emphysema or something. People who didn't know him thought this 'old man's going down.' So, we're all eating, and Diamond starts one of his coughing fits. The whole diner turns to stare, horrified. Meanwhile, we're just eating like nothing's happening. 'Hey Jim, pass the salt.' 'Michael, hand me the ketchup.' The waitresses must've thought, 'These guys are heartless assholes.' This happened everywhere we went. But for us, it was just another day."

By now, Cousin was dying laughing.

I waited for him to catch his breath, then continued.

"So, we finish eating, and Diamond calls the waitress over. 'Darling, give me the check.' Back then, you could call a lady 'darling' without getting your fucking head ripped off. Anyway, he gets the check and says, 'Mikey, go tell the guys to head to the car. I'll meet you, just gotta hit the bathroom.' I said, 'Okay, Diamond, all good.' Having no idea what the crazy fuck was up to.

Five minutes later, he walks out all casual, hops in the car, and says, 'Let's go.' Off we went. Only later did we find out that he snuck out, beat the check, and swiped a bunch of candy from the front counter. His pockets were *stuffed*. He had more candy in his pocket than a kid on Halloween. Can't make this shit up. And we were lucky we didn't wind up in a jail cell next to my father."

Cousin was practically crying from laughter.

"Diamond was probably in his early seventies then. Doesn't he remind you of the sweet, kind old grandpa you see on TV?"

Diamond...

Like Cousin, I loved Diamond. In time, I became his number one grandchild. When I was around seven, we lived with him and my grandmother in Jackson Heights. Every night, he'd be in the next room, screaming into the phone, arguing about something. Meanwhile, I'd be watching reruns of *I Love Lucy*, convinced his problems were insurmountable.

Then, after hanging up, he'd walk into my room, smile, and act like everything was great. He never carried that stress over to me. Maybe it was his way of protecting me, reassuring me. It stuck with me, and I always appreciated that.

Diamond was nuts. But he was lovable. My mother adored him, despite all his insanity.

There's not a day that goes by that I don't think about him.

After an hour of Diamond stories, wiping away laughter-induced tears, we got back in the car. Nothing like a good Diamond story to distract from the sadness that loomed ahead.

Cousin took the wheel, and off we went, continuing our Road Trip.

4

The Tape

Back on the road around nine, Cousin is driving, and I gotta watch him like a hawk. The guy thinks he's in the Indianapolis 500. We're somewhere in South Jersey, and these roads are crawling with highway patrol.

A couple of years back, Grace and I took a similar road trip down to North Carolina. My father had been transferred to the federal prison in Butner after being diagnosed with prostate cancer. He needed surgery, and the facility doubles as a medical center. Years later, Bernie Madoff would end up there too. Guess misery loves company.

That trip, my cousin was behind the wheel while Grace and I dozed off. Bad idea. He was pushing ninety-one in a sixty-five, right in the heart of Virginia where the troopers don't mess around. Seeing New York plates? That just made their eyes light up like a Christmas tree. Next thing I knew, sirens and flashing lights jolted us awake. My first thought? *Yeah, this isn't gonna end well.*

Out-of-state plates always get the same question: Where you headed? And let's be real—you can't just say, "Oh, just swinging by the federal prison to visit my felon father." That wouldn't exactly earn us a warning and smile.

Luckily, Grace was riding shotgun. The moment the trooper stepped out, hand hovering near his gun, she took the lead. And thank God for that. I was in the backseat, bracing for the worst.

Grace is a knockout with light brown hair, hazel eyes, and the kind of effortless charm that can diffuse a situation in seconds. She's also sharp as hell. Hey, we're New Yorkers, it's in our DNA. She's five years younger than me, my so-called 'partner in crime'—though let's keep that off the record.

She's got this natural instinct to take care of people, and I count myself lucky that she's my sister. I've always believed God gifts us angels, and for me, she's right up there with my wife and mother. Funny thing about tough times—you figure out who you want in the trenches with you. And Grace? She's exactly that person.

The officer strolled up to the car, taking his sweet time. I still remember the name on his badge, Romano. *Alright,* I thought, *he's Italian. We got a shot.*

Grace, always quick on her feet, put on her best innocent act and spun a story about how we were on our way to Norfolk Naval Station to visit her fiancé. Quite the creative detour from our actual destination, a federal prison. But wouldn't you know it? It worked.

Officer Romano still asked for my cousin's license and registration, which, by some miracle, came back clean. He even congratulated Grace on the "upcoming wedding." Guess he had a soft spot for the military. Score one for the Navy!

Back to Route 80...

South Jersey is nothing like the Jersey we know—Hoboken, Fort Lee, Jersey City, places just a stone's throw from Manhattan. Those spots feel like New York. South Jersey? Whole different world. We might as well be in Iowa. The vibe shifts completely, and even the accents pick up a little twang.

For once, my cousin was driving the speed limit. Thank you, Lord. No imminent threats on the horizon.

David was in the back seat, and as usual on these trips, he started with his go-to opener, "Hey, remember when so-and-so..."

David's only eighteen months older than me, so we practically grew up attached at the hip. Like I mentioned before, he also had his fair share of battles with the life we were dealt. We walked a lot of the same roads, fought some of the same struggles.

Brotherhood can be complicated, ego, bravado, competition, and, let's be honest, a sprinkle of insecurity. Ours wasn't much different. But no matter what, we were bound by the shared struggle of living up to our mother's expectations. It's like soldiers who make it through war together; you never forget the battles, and you never lose the bond or the love.

David suddenly yelled, "Hey, Michael, tell Cousin about Nino's father's tape!"

Cousin, looking confused, squinted at me. "What do ya mean, *tape?*"

Before I get into the story, let me paint a picture of Nino and his old man.

Nino's father was the maître d' at The Plaza Hotel in New York City. Quiet guy, thick Italian accent, always carried himself with a calm, easy-going demeanor. He worked nights, and every morning before crashing, he'd empty his pockets and leave all his cash tips stacked neatly on his dresser.

Well, Nino had *itchy* fingers. Every day, like clockwork, he'd slip into his father's bedroom and skim ten, maybe twenty bucks off the top. Just enough to keep himself flush with cash but not enough for his old man to notice. And back in the '70s? That was *serious* money for a kid.

I'd tell Nino, "I'm starving. Let's hit the Italian deli for some heroes."

Without hesitation, he'd run upstairs, dip into the stash, and come back with a fistful of dollars. We'd eat like kings. We got whatever we wanted—sandwiches, records, ice cream—you name it, we got it.

Nino was fucking nuts. Dropped out in the tenth grade, never set foot in school again. But I'll tell you, he was a blast to hang out with. By twelve, he was chain-smoking like a grizzled old man and downing Cokes™ like water. He lived right on my block, which was shaped like a horseshoe, and was one of "our crew" I mentioned earlier.

And in his ample free time, he had a little side hustle. He'd sneak into the local candy store and swipe what we called back in the '70s girly magazines. Had to steal them, of course, because lunatic Nino was too young to buy them.

Now, let's be honest. We all loved those magazines. Guilty as charged. But these weren't *Playboys*. Nah, those were practically *wholesome* compared to what this lunatic lifted. This maniac went straight for the hardcore ones—the kind with all the action shots, if you catch my drift.

And when you're thirteen or fourteen years old? That's heaven. Looking back, life was so damn innocent back then.

Now, back to the story…

"Cousin, the tape was an eight-millimeter film I found in Nino's father's car. You know, back in the day, whether it was audio or video, everything was recorded and played on tape, actual reels of film."

"I was thirteen, Nino was fourteen, and it was a late summer afternoon. We were just hanging in the park, bored out of our minds, when we decided to head across the street to his house for a bite. His father, who had worked all night, was upstairs knocked out cold, sleeping."

"His car was parked in the garage, and for kicks, we climbed inside and started pretending to drive. I was in the passenger seat, messing around, when I accidentally kicked open the glove compartment. And that's when a reel of film tumbled out...*the tape.*"

"I picked it up, turning it over in my hands. 'Nino, what the fuck is this?'"

"He had no clue. Probably embarrassed since, well, it came straight from his father's car. Curious, I pulled it out of the white box and unraveled a section of the film, holding it up to the light. And what did I see? Everything. Just like the raunchy magazines he used to swipe, but this time? This time, it could *come to life.*"

"My heart started pounding. Holy shit, I thought. Thirteen years old and about to watch this? I turned to Nino, wide-eyed. 'Nino, we just hit the fucking lotto!' I have an old movie projector in my basement. 'Let's go.' Nino was *all in.* Sure, he might've been embarrassed, but let's be real—he lived for this kind of shit. The kid had more dirty magazines stashed in his house than Hugh Hefner."

"We booked it five houses down to my place. My mother was upstairs, so I yelled up, 'Hey Ma, I'm here with Nino. We're heading to the basement to watch *The Honeymooners* on the projector!'"

"Clueless as ever, she just called back, 'Okay, enjoy!'"

"Cousin, listen. I was *desperate* to watch this tape. Desperate enough to risk my mother walking in and catching us. And you *know* your aunt. If she caught me watching this, I wouldn't just be grounded. I'd be dead."

"We ran downstairs, and I set everything up. The projector, the screen. I was shaking with excitement. Nino was right there with me, practically vibrating. But then...problem."

"When I went to load the reel onto the projector, the tape kept slipping. It wouldn't catch properly, wouldn't move along the wheel. And then...disaster."

"The projector's bulb, the one that illuminates the film? It started *burning* the tape. For a second, we just stared. Then Nino panicked. 'Oh *fuck*! My father's tape!'"

"That was it. We knew we had the wrong projector. The dream was over. We packed everything up and bolted."

As we headed upstairs, I shouted, 'Ma, we're leaving!'"

"She called back, 'How was the show?'"

"Without missing a beat, I yelled, 'It was great! Thanks!'"

This Wasn't Over. We Were on a Mission!

"Cousin, there was *no way* we were letting this end like that. We had to watch the tape. So, we headed back to the park, carrying our prized possession like the Holy Grail. Our crew was there. Dave, Swaggy, Sal, and Duck. I told them the whole story. Poor Nino. It was his father's tape, but by that point, he didn't give a shit. His degenerate side had fully taken over; he just wanted to see it through."

"Duck, always the problem-solver, swore he had a projector at his house. That was all we needed to hear, and we were back in business."

Now, a quick sidebar on Duck. He got his nickname because, for some bizarre reason, he started losing clumps of hair as a kid. He claimed it was from a Halloween prank, that some asshole put hair removal cream in his hair instead of shaving cream. Whether that was true or not, nobody ever pushed the issue.

But the real kicker? He didn't just lose hair; he started *plucking out* his own eyelashes. Not his eyebrows. His eyelashes!

So now, picture this: a balding kid with no eyelashes. I took one look at him and said, "You look like a duck," and boom. That was it. Christened. Duck was born. Thankfully, it wasn't some illness, because let me tell you, Duck kept quacking for a long time, if you catch my drift.

Back to the tape.

"Duck lived about five houses from Nino, ten from me. We walked in, same routine. He yelled up to his mom, 'Hey Ma, I'm here with the guys. We're gonna watch *The Honeymooners* on the projector.'"

She hollered back, 'Okay, have fun!'"

"By this point, my heart was pounding a hundred miles an hour."

"His house was laid out differently than mine. No basement, just a small den, or what some people call a family room, right near the front door. We shut the door, and it was go time.
That's when we hit another snag, no screen.

"At first, we panicked. Then Swaggy, the smoothest of us all, came through. 'Fuck it, pull down the window shade. We'll use that.'"

Genius.

"Now, Cousin, you know Corona. The houses are *right* on top of each other, maybe twenty feet apart. Duck had two younger sisters who kept busting our balls, trying to come inside and watch *The Honeymooners*. Duck kept yelling at them to get lost."

"We knew we were playing with fire. His mom was right upstairs, and she could come down at *any moment*. But we didn't care. We had a winning lottery ticket, and we were damn well cashing it in."

Showtime

"By now, the sun was setting. It was almost dark. Perfect conditions."

"We set up the projector, loaded the reel, and the tape began to play. Cousin, it showed everything. And I mean *everything*."

"We were a bunch of thirteen-to-fifteen-year-old kids. It was impossible to contain our excitement. We were giggling, yelling, oohing, and ahhing at the screen. Ten minutes in, disaster struck."

"Duck's mother came flying down the stairs, screaming, 'OPEN THIS DOOR! WHAT ARE YOU WATCHING?!'"

"Duck, thinking fast, yelled back, 'Ma! It's *The Honeymooners!*'"

"As she started rattling the door, I panicked. 'Rewind it! Take it off the reel! Hide it!'
Wouldn't you know, the projector didn't have a rewind button."

"Instead, the tape got stuck on the reel, and the projector's bulb started burning it. Again."

"Duck's mom was pounding on the door."

"We were desperate. I yelled, 'FUCK IT! Cut the tape! Take it off the reel!'"

"Nino, in full panic mode, screamed, 'NO! DON'T CUT *THE TAPE*! IT'S MY FATHER'S!'"

"Too late. We had no choice. The door burst open. Duck's mother stormed in, with the tape still on the reel. She demanded we leave the room!"

"Two seconds later, a scream erupted that could be heard in Canarsie. 'YOU *PIGS*!'"

"She came storming out. 'WHERE DID YOU GET THIS?! WHOSE TAPE IS THIS?'"

Without hesitation, *we all* shouted, except Nino, 'IT'S NINO'S FATHER'S!' And then the final twist of fate."

"What we hadn't realized—what *none* of us noticed—was that when we played the tape on the window shade, it wasn't just showing inside the room. It was projecting onto the entire side of the next-door neighbor's house. For the *entire block* to see."

"Cousin, you *know* Corona. Nobody sits in their backyards. The Italians all sit in their garages, out front of the house, just hanging out."

"Well, that night, they were accidentally treated to a giant, XXX-rated drive-in movie. That night, the entire neighborhood watched the tape. We were the talk of the block!"

I hope the neighbors enjoyed that ten minutes as much as we did...

The Aftermath

"The next day, we got word that Duck's mother marched over to Nino's house with the tape in hand, and handed it straight to his mother. His poor fucking dad. Can you imagine?"

"Now, Nino's mom was a sweetheart, but she was also a crazy Sicilian. Tiny woman, maybe five feet tall, with blonde hair that looked like it was held together by an entire can of hairspray.

She worked as an aide in a nursing home—not a beautician, not a hairdresser. But whenever Nino got caught doing something stupid, she had a *very specific* punishment. She'd grab a pair of paper-cutting scissors and butcher his hair."

"This wasn't a one-time thing, either. It happened all the time."

"So whenever Nino came out looking like a blind man hacked at his head, we knew exactly what went down."

"Cuz, after THE TAPE INCIDENT, we didn't see Nino for a week. And when we finally did? His hair looked like some deranged lunatic went at it with a weed whacker. It was bad."

"We lost it. Laughed so hard we could barely breathe."

"Nino? He didn't say much. Just looked at us, shook his head, and muttered the same two words he always did. 'Fuck you.'"

"That was it. Classic Nino."

Dodging a Bullet

Thank God Duck's mother never came to my house and told my mom.

I spent that entire week on edge, convinced she was going to show up at any moment. Felt like the longest week of my life.

But I lived to tell the tale, all thanks to Duck's mom keeping her mouth shut.

As for what happened to Nino's father?

No clue. Never found out. Oh well.

The Road Trip Continues

The three of us were dying laughing by this point.

Cousin was laughing so hard he almost drove off the road.

Because sometimes, when life throws heavy shit your way, laughter is the antidote. It keeps your mind off the inevitable, gives you a break from reality.

With that, we pulled into a rest stop to stretch our legs, hit the bathroom, and grab some air. The only thought in mind, The Tape.

5

Kunta Kinte

WHAT's a Kunta Kinte? Who's Kunta Kinte? Well, let me tell you.

Kunta Kinte was a fictional character from a groundbreaking TV miniseries in the late 1970s. The show was called *Roots*, and at the time, it was huge. It followed the story of an African man and his descendants who were sold into slavery in America—a brutal, shameful stain on American history.

There's one scene that sticks out in particular. Kunta Kinte tries to escape his plantation, running for his life, but he gets caught. To make sure he *never* tries to escape again, his master orders the front half of his right foot to be cut off.

Brutal.

On the Road Again

We sat at the rest stop for about fifteen minutes. Nothing fancy, just a no-frills industrial building with bathrooms and gas pumps out front. Like every other rest stop, it had vending machines, so we loaded up on potato chips, cookies, and gum.

Screw any hard candy. I wasn't going through *that* again.

I had already punched the prison address into the GPS, so we had a rough idea of our ETA. Made me think that back in the day, we didn't have navigation in cars. You used a map. That was it.

I never would have imagined, back in the eighties, that one day cars would have a voice-activated system barking out directions. Crazy.

I was back behind the wheel, and the GPS sent us straight onto Route 80. We had to stay on that highway for *at least* a hundred miles. Before long, Cousin and Dave knocked out, leaving me alone with the radio.

Now, when you're on a long drive, if you find a good station, you don't change it. You hold on to it for dear life because the second you start flipping around, you're guaranteed to lose the only station you actually liked.

After fumbling around, I finally landed on a solid rock station. Perfect. Just me, the road, and the music.

And then, "Photograph" by Ringo Starr came on.

For all you Gen Z'ers out there, Ringo was the drummer for a little band called The Beatles.

Funny thing about music, it's like a time machine. One song can take you right back to a specific moment in your life. And that song?

That song took me straight back to the early to mid-seventies.

The place? My father's pizzerias.

Which, of course, he owned with Diamond.

A Trip Down Memory Lane

As I'm driving, my time machine takes me away...

My father and Diamond owned two pizzerias, both in downtown Manhattan. One was on the corner of Canal Street and the Avenue of the Americas, now part of Soho. The other was at North Moore and Greenwich, now smack in the middle of Tribeca.

Today, those areas are upscale, trendy, and wildly expensive. But back in the 1970s? They were gritty, rundown, and dangerous.

To survive, you had to have your head on a swivel. The city was a *different* place back then.

In 1975, President Gerald Ford came to New York. The city was teetering on bankruptcy and desperate for federal aid. The response? Ford basically told New York to drop dead. It was plastered on the front page of every newspaper. The city was a mess.

Before the pizza business, my father was working in the plumber's union after a failed attempt at running a bar/lounge (we'll get to that later). When New York didn't get the bailout, all hell broke loose. Construction came to a halt, jobs dried up, and my father was one of many who got laid off.

The Hustler

But my father wasn't one to sit around and sulk. He was a survivor. He started doing what we called "side jobs"—plumbing gigs on the side, with his younger cousin Johnny as his assistant. My father was good. He wasn't a "shoemaker."

Now, for those unfamiliar, a "shoemaker" in street lingo is someone who's terrible at their trade. If you hired a plumber and heard someone say, "Don't hire him, he's a fucking shoemaker," you knew to run the other way.

My father was the opposite.

Word of his solid work spread, and he connected with Mr. Schwartz, a wealthy building owner in Manhattan. Whenever one of Schwartz's buildings had plumbing issues, he'd call my dad. It wasn't glamorous, but it paid the bills, and I remember being relieved that we didn't have to sell our house in Corona. We had only been there for about three years, and the thought of losing it scared the hell out of me. I loved Corona!

But my father was never content with "just getting by." He always wanted more. He was confident, dependable, and fearless when it came to chasing new opportunities. It's a trait I inherited from him, and it's helped me "earn my stripes" in life. As I mentioned earlier, he was the kind of guy you wanted in a foxhole with you.

He was on the right track, making a living, paying the bills. But life is funny like that. Eventually, he found himself at a crossroads, forced to choose between the stable, practical path and the one that offered intrigue, risk, and power. He chose the latter.

And as Robert Frost once said, "that has made all the difference."

Grace Pizza Is Born

One day, a unique opportunity came his way. He and Diamond bought a pizza place from a guy who was practically giving it away. Tragically, the owner's young son had lost his hand in the dough mixer, and the man just wanted out. My father and Diamond, knowing nothing about making pizza or running a restaurant, jumped on the chance. It was a leap of faith.

The first location was on Canal Street, and they named it Grace Pizza after my sister. It was the mid-seventies, and my brother and

I worked there from a young age, learning "the trade." We were just kids—eleven and thirteen—but soon enough, we were making dough, flipping pizzas, and running the shop like seasoned pros.

It was a hell of an education. I felt like I was eleven going on thirty-one. Working there taught me responsibility, street smarts, and how to deal with *all* types of people. The lessons I learned in that pizzeria were as valuable as any Ivy League education.

Street Justice

Now, Canal Street wasn't exactly Disneyland™ back then. When we first opened, we had a steady stream of people with bad intentions—guys who'd come in, buy something, and then refuse to pay or just cause chaos. They figured they could get away with it.

They figured wrong.

Behind the counter, we kept three or four baseball bats. My family weren't ballplayers, if you catch my drift. My father and Diamond weren't afraid to enforce a little street justice when necessary. Diamond, who was in his mid-sixties at the time, was Babe Ruth, and my father was Lou Gehrig. I can still see them in my mind, chasing down the jerkoffs and "adjusting their attitudes" with those bats.

Word spread fast. Within a few months, Grace Pizza went from being a target to being the safest place on Canal Street. STREET JUSTICE!

A Different World

The world's a different place today. Try standing up for yourself now, and you'll end up in jail.

But back then? You fought for what was yours.

And honestly?

Those were the good old days.

The Unwritten Rule

My father had a strict policy: Every cop that walked into Grace Pizza did not pay. That was the rule.

Now, my father and Diamond weren't exactly law-abiding citizens, but they respected the fact that these guys were just doing their jobs. And in return, the cops respected them. Over time, they built a solid relationship, a mutual understanding of common courtesy.

They knew us. We knew them.

And when we closed up at night, those same cops kept an eye on the place, made sure *nobody* messed with it. It was appreciated, and I learned an important lesson: If you show respect and courtesy most times, it comes right back to you. That unspoken rule is something I carry with me to this day.

Over time, Grace Pizza became a success, and eventually, they opened another store eight blocks away—Grace 2. That's where I ended up working, and by the time I was fourteen, I was co-managing the place.

I still remember making deliveries at night, navigating those dark, unpredictable streets. But no matter how rough it was, I always felt a strange sense of comfort.

Why?

Because just seven blocks away, the twin towers of the World Trade Center stood tall.

Their office lights glowed like a giant nightlight in the sky. To me, they were like a massive security blanket, watching over the city, watching over me.

A Day at Grace 1

One summer afternoon, I was working at Grace 1.

It was the usual lunchtime madness—lines out the door, phones ringing off the hook, orders coming in nonstop. Delivery and pickup orders were a huge slice of our revenue (no pun intended). We were surrounded by office buildings, and the lunch crowd was our bread and butter.

It became a tremendous success.

Grace 1 had perfect hours, open at 10 a.m., close by 6 p.m. That made it the go-to pizza joint in the neighborhood.

But here's the thing about Manhattan: There's nowhere to park. Even back in the seventies, it was impossible.

Luckily, my father had his spot.

Right on the side of the pizzeria was a small cul-de-sac next to a park with basketball courts. He *always* parked there. And thanks to our relationship with the local cops, he never got a ticket.

Until that day.

Kunta Kinte

We were so slammed that we didn't notice what was happening outside.

A meter maid had pulled up on his scooter and started writing a ticket for my father's car.

Now, for those unfamiliar, a meter maid is a city worker whose entire job is writing parking tickets. They are NOT cops. And let me tell you that everybody in New York hates meter maids.

They take so much abuse; it's practically in the job description.

I was behind the counter with Diamond. He was working the register, as usual. That was his thing. He handled the cash. Surprised?

From the corner of my eye, I saw the guy step off his scooter.

Tall, Black guy, probably in his forties, wearing the standard brown uniform. He casually pulled out his ticket book and started circling my father's car, jotting down the plate number.

That's when I lost it.

"Diamond! This fucking guy is giving my father a ticket!"

My father was in the back, completely oblivious.

But Diamond? He snapped.

Before I could even count to three, he started banging on the window, trying to scare the guy off. The meter maid glanced over, completely unfazed, and gave this little wave like he was shooing away a fly.

That's all it took.

An atom bomb went off.

Diamond bolted out of the pizzeria, yelling, cursing up a storm.

A New York Standoff

The guy just ignored him and kept writing.

I ran to the back and told my father what was happening. Within seconds, we were both outside.

By the time we got there, Diamond was going fucking nuts.

"You motherfucker! We know *every* cop in the first precinct! Go ask anyone who we are!"

I have to give the guy credit—he did not care. Didn't matter if we knew the mayor. Didn't matter if we knew the Pope. He just kept writing that ticket.

That's when Diamond completely lost it.

He grabbed the guy by the throat and started choking him, screaming, "YOU BLACK COCKSUCKER! I'LL CUT YOUR FOOT OFF LIKE KUNTA KINTE!"

Now, I know. That's racist as hell, and there's no excuse for it.

Those were the times. That was *that* generation.

We jumped on Diamond and pried him off the guy.

The meter maid—now officially Kunta Kinte in our family—grabbed his walkie-talkie and called for backup.

Within a minute, at least five cop cars rolled up.

They had no idea what was going on; they just knew there was a 9-1-1 call.

They jumped out, ready to handle the situation.

Then they saw us.

And they started laughing.

They knew the players.

The cops pulled Kunta to the side and smoothed everything over. Anybody else would've been arrested on the spot. But because it was us?

They squashed it. Thank you NYPD! Much respect!

And wouldn't you know it? We never saw that meter maid ever again.

From that day on, Kunta Kinte became a household name in our family.

Just Another Day at Grace Pizza

The police were very familiar with both of our pizza shops.

Cops getting called to Grace 1 or Grace 2? Routine.

Take this one time. Diamond was alone in the store early in the morning. Sometimes, he'd open early for the Catholic school down the block.

That day, there were a bunch of female students inside when a homeless guy decided to stand right in front of the store and start pissing on the sidewalk.

Diamond wasn't having it.

He knocked on the window, motioning for the guy to fucking move on.

The guy looked right at him and said, "Fuck off."

That was a mistake.

Diamond stormed outside and *knocked* the guy out cold. Keep in mind, he was sixty-five years old at the time.

Later, I remember him shaking his hand, complaining, "Mikey, my gout is acting up. My fucking hand is killing me."

I laughed. "Gout? Yeah, I'm sure knocking that guy out had nothing to do with it."

Cops were called for that one.

Broadway and Baseball Bats

Another time at Grace 2, a guy came strolling down the street—completely naked—on a Saturday morning.

Just walking along, like it was the most normal thing in the world.

Now my mom happened to be there that day, along with my aunt and Uncle Rich. They were all dressed up, about to head out for a Broadway® show or something.

Well, my father and Uncle Rich saw this naked lunatic and didn't hesitate for a second. They grabbed baseball bats and chased that piece of shit down the street.

Cops were called for that one too.

Just Another Day in Paradise...

Shit like this happened all the time.

For most people, this would be insanity. For us? Just another day.

As a teenager, I didn't question any of it. It was normal. People say you become the person you are based on the people you're surrounded by.

Well, this was my world.

And to be totally honest? At the time, I loved it.

I mean, really—how could you not?

Today I live a productive and constructive life, and I learned my lessons well and applied them. However, if I'm *really* being honest,

I kind of still love it, a touch of that "element" is still in me today and therein lies the rub.

The Punchline

Finally, Cousin and Dave woke up.

I was tired of driving and needed a break. They stretched, rubbed their eyes, and then noticed the huge grin on my face.

Cousin squinted at me. "What the fuck are you laughing at?"

I chuckled. "Nothing, really."

I let it sit for about five seconds, then smirked and asked, "Hey...you remember that show, *Roots*?" I paused for effect.

Kunta Kinte?

6

A Day at the Races

We pulled over for a quick five-minute stop to use the restroom, and then it was "back in the saddle." With my brother at the wheel, we were officially in Pennsylvania, with eighty-nine miles to Lewisburg, according to the GPS.

Pennsylvania's rolling hills were a sight for sore eyes, especially for three boys from Queens. There was something about the landscape, the sheer openness of it, that filled me with a rare sense of peace. I never realized how many horse farms dotted this part of the state. Acres and acres of lush green fields stretched out before us, framed by white picket fences and weathered barns. Horses grazed lazily, unbothered by time.

The scene was beautiful.

Unforgettable.

And yet, as I stared out the window, I felt the weight of something heavier than the horizon. This was the last trip. The finality of it hit me like a punch to the gut. I wasn't ready, but there was no stopping what was coming. My mind began its own journey, spiraling into the hours ahead, trying to brace for the inevitable.

Losing someone suddenly leaves you with an emptiness that's impossible to put into words.
How am I supposed to act?
How is this going to change my life?
How will this affect my family?
Is it okay to laugh at memories that once brought so much joy when the present is drowning in sorrow?

A road trip like this should be about fun—about sharing laughter and stories. But this wasn't just any trip.

As we passed another stretch of horse farms, my thoughts drifted to my father. Happy memories. Sad ones. I didn't want to drown in grief but how could I not, knowing how his story ended?

A jail cell is not a place to die with dignity. It's a place where you die alone, without family, without love, without a shred of compassion. That's not how it's supposed to happen. No one comes into this world destined for that kind of ending.

How do you wind up on a road that dead-ends in a prison cell?

No matter how much you love someone, no matter how deeply they're embedded in your life, you can't help but wonder: *Didn't they see where they were headed? Why couldn't they change course?*

Life presents us all with forks in the road. Choices. My father had his share, and yet it appeared to me he was unable to change his road of choice. Once committed, there was no coming back.

Maybe he didn't have the right people around him—people who could have spoken to his mind, to his soul, and pulled him in a different direction.

I'll never know.

What I *do* know is that my mother never gave up on me. She taught me that believing in yourself is half the battle. She made me understand that greatness exists within all of us—it's just a matter of digging deep and working for it. I never questioned whether I'd end up in the "winner's circle."

Second place? Not an option.

And by the way, when I say "second place," I'm not talking about money or success in the way most people define it. The *real* winners are the ones who live up to their potential, who don't waste the gifts they've been given. What does the winner's circle look like? That's different for everyone. I will leave that up to you to decide.

My father should have been in that circle. He had the character, the abilities. He had everything it took.

As we continued along Route 80, my mind spun in circles, tangled in frustration, exhaustion, and the nagging *why* of it all. Eventually, the weight of it pulled me under, and I drifted off to sleep.

The Reason We Dream

Dreams consolidate our memories. They're how we manage and process emotions. They tend to align with whatever's swirling around in our minds, reflecting our present mental state. This particular dream was so vivid, so real, it pulled me straight back to 1977.

It started with those beautiful horses in the fields.

Reminiscing Dream – Garment Center, NYC, 1977

By this time, in addition to the pizzerias, my father was part-owner of a thriving garment manufacturing and design company called Classic Fit. He had been introduced to the business by my uncle, who connected him with a successful operator in the industry. The garment trade—known in those days as the rag business—was its own wild, fast-paced world.

Once again, my father trusted his instincts, took a leap of faith, and found success.

Now, let's be clear: He didn't know a damn thing about making clothes. The extent of his experience ended at *wearing* them. Yet here he was, designing, producing, marketing, and selling apparel across the country. His new partner, Ben, was the real expert. He was sharp, articulate, and, unlike my father and uncle, he was Jewish.

Not that it mattered; it was actually refreshing. Ben brought a new dimension into our world. I admired him. Respected him. They say Italians and Jews make a great team, and I couldn't agree more.

Not long after, my father faced a decision that would change the course of not just his life but all of ours.

The truth is he had always been drawn—no, pulled—toward a certain kind of lifestyle. It had been around him since he was a kid, woven into the fabric of his world. It was as alluring as a beautiful woman, as addictive as the strongest drug. And just like steel to a magnet, he couldn't resist it.

Around this time, he stood at a crossroads. Two roads stretched out before him. One led to a steady business, stability, and a future. The other led to glamour, power, and everything that came with it.

He chose the latter.

And after that choice, everything changed.

With his new sense of status came a new level of respect. He carried himself differently. He was no longer involved in the day-to-day operations of the pizzerias. My brother and I were still in high school, my sister was in junior high. We weren't in a position to step in and manage the stores, so he sold them.

If it had been me? I would've thought long-term. I would've held onto the properties, built wealth, and created something lasting for future generations. But my father wasn't built that way. He lived for the now.

He was famous for saying, "Money's only paper with dead people on them."

Planning for the future? That wasn't in his playbook.

I see life like a game of chess; you don't just move the piece in front of you. You think three steps ahead. That's how you win. That's how you earn your spot in the winner's circle.

My mother understood that. She taught us to be patient, to think ahead, to always do the right thing. She instilled in us the importance of playing the long game. And for that, I will always be grateful.

But my father? Who influenced him?

Diamond?

Looking back now, those two pizzerias were in neighborhoods that have since become some of the trendiest, most expensive areas in New York City. The real estate is untouchable. Back in the seventies, those properties could've been bought for the price of a pack of gum.

Oh well. Hindsight is always twenty-twenty. Whatever business my father developed became wildly successful! He always seemed to have a special touch, and it appeared to me luck was never on his side. Outside influences seemed to always derail him.

And just like that, the same theme played out once again—second place.

The Rag Business

I have to admit that the rag business was a hell of a lot more interesting and definitely sexier than slinging pizzas.

We designed women's budget blouses, meaning they were stylish yet affordable for most people. Our team was small but efficient. Ben's wife was our blouse designer, and we had two seamstresses and three sales reps. The reps' job was to take our samples and sell them to buyers from major department stores and smaller chains across the country.

I worked in the shipping department, making sure every order got out on time. My brother handled purchasing, sourcing fabrics, buttons, and trims for our designs. Grace was still in high school, but I had no doubt she would've been a natural-born salesperson. She had that fire in her.

Classic Fit took off fast thanks to Ben's knowledge and experience. But my father? He had his own role.

He was there to protect the company's interests and to make sure no one tried to step in and stake a claim.

See, business in New York isn't always just business. There are layers. Hidden aspects. Unwritten rules. And in that world, protection wasn't just a concept, it was a necessity.

Then there was my uncle. Larger than life. Loud. Always making his presence known. But the truth? He was trouble. Nothing but.

Remember what I said about loyalty?

The Other Side of the Business

Over time, my father found himself involved in other ventures beyond Classic Fit. The garment industry was filled with sharp, streetwise characters—people who, while not exactly Harvard grads, knew how to play the game. Many of them had their vices. Some liked to gamble. Some indulged in those long martini lunches. And some? Well, let's just say they enjoyed action of all kinds.

To survive in the rag business, you had to create your own thunder. With that came stress, and stress needed an outlet.

My father? He was happy to provide one.

He had two or three so-called "assistants" who helped him collect the steady flow of money that started pouring in.

My mother? She hated it.

She saw it for what it was and warned me about it constantly. She never stopped fighting for my soul, reminding me that no matter how intoxicating it all seemed, it wasn't the path to the winner's circle.

The Sport of Kings

Ben loved thoroughbreds—their grace, their power. He owned them, bred them, and admired them as the magnificent creatures they were.

My father? He loved them too just in a different way.

For him, and especially for Diamond, horses weren't just animals. They were bets. Action. The track was their playground.

I have to admit that I loved going with them. There was something electric about Belmont and Aqueduct in the seventies. Horse racing was The Sport of Kings.

We were the maniacs screaming at the top of our lungs, either at the live race in front of us or at the TV screens inside the track. It was a rush!

I was fifteen when I learned how to read the racing form.

My father, uncle, and Ben never sat in the grandstands with the regular crowd. They had a spot in the restaurant, a home base for watching the races, making bets, and soaking up the action.

And, of course, Diamond was always there.

Another TKO

One afternoon, we were all in the restaurant when a voice suddenly crackled over the loudspeaker, "Can the family of Vinny Diamond please report to security?"

We froze.

Vinny Diamond?

What the fuck?

Turns out, Diamond was trying to get a bet in. The window was about to close—he had maybe sixty seconds left. If you don't place your bet before the race starts, you're out.

According to him, some "Asian guy" cut in front of him, blocking his shot at getting the bet in on time.

So, naturally, Diamond did what Diamond does. He knocked the guy out cold right there in the middle of the grandstand.

Oh, and did I mention? He was sixty-seven years old at the time.

My father went to security and somehow managed to smooth things over. No arrest. No major fallout. Just another day in the life.

When my father came back to the restaurant, I turned to Diamond.

"Diamond, what the hell happened?"

He looked at me, dead serious, and said, "Mikey, this fucking Chinaman (yeah, I know racist) cut in line while I was trying to get my bet in. So, I knocked him the fuck out."

Then he shook his head and muttered, "Cocksucker."

Sixty-seven years old. I can still hear his voice today.

Can't make this shit up.

Lotta Dust and Sols Venture

Over time, my father and Ben took their love of horse racing to the next level, and they started owning racehorses. Their first horse was named Lotta Dust, a name we always got a kick out of because, well, it was perfect. The damn horse came in last every single time, eating the dust of every competitor in front of him.

But then came Sols Venture, a different story entirely. Sols was competitive, held his own, and actually gave us something to root for.

Now, my father and Ben weren't just gamblers at the track anymore. They were in the horse racing business. They formed a stable under the name BANT Stables, a combination of both their first names. They hired a trainer, got their horses in shape, and they were off to the races.

Dream Interruption

Suddenly, I felt a nudge.

It was Cousin. "Hey, you would know. Who played third base for the 1976 Cincinnati Reds?"

Half-asleep, I muttered, "Pete Rose, you stupid fuck," rolled over, and within thirty seconds, I was back out cold.

The Dream Continues

My father and Ben, always ones to have a little fun, designed the jockey's racing silks in a way that became legendary at the track. The shirt a jockey wears is called "jockey's silks," and theirs was a statement piece.

The silk featured the Italian flag and right in the center of the back was a big-ass Star of David.

People *loved* it.

Every time Sols Venture hit the track, the crowd went wild. The jockey would ride out, and you'd hear hoots and hollers from all around the grandstand and restaurant. He became the horse to watch.

Unlike Lotta Dust, Sols Venture was actually in the mix. He came in fourth a couple of times and even placed third once, a big deal in the racing world. Every time he ran, we were all in. Just hearing the race announcer call his name gave us a rush.

Those were good times. And I was right in the middle of it.

The Race of a Lifetime

Then came *the* race.

It was a chilly November afternoon at Aqueduct Racetrack, right in Queens, the only racetrack in New York City. Built in 1894, it was no Belmont or Saratoga. There was no elegance, no frills.

It was pure, unfiltered degenerate gambler territory. And the hardcore bettors loved it.

That day we were sitting in the restaurant, and at the table next to us was a major league baseball manager—a well-known guy—with two of his players.

Sol's Venture was scheduled to run in the seventh race.

Since I was the designated runner, I placed bets for everyone at our table. I was constantly weaving in and out of the big glass doors at the restaurant entrance, running bets to the windows.

I was wearing my New York Yankees 1977 Championship T-shirt, which, apparently, was a trigger for the manager.

Every time I passed his table, he'd throw me a thumbs-down and yell, "Hey kid, the Yankees stink!"

This went on for three races straight.

Finally, my uncle—who had the gift of gab—invited him and his players over.

The guy was Italian, so naturally, he fit right in. Within minutes, it was like we'd known him forever.

All in on Sols

The sixth race ended.

Now it was Sol's Venture's turn.

Between races, you get about twenty-five minutes to analyze the racing forms, read the tip sheets, and place bets. For us? No analysis needed. It was Sols Venture to win.

God only knows how much money my father, uncle, and Ben threw down.

Diamond, true to form, told me, "Kid, I put everything I had on me on this one."

Even the major league manager and his players got in on it.

Seeing all this action, I figured fuck it, and I put down whatever I had in my pocket.

Sols had run a strong race last time out, and this was a weaker field. He should be a shoo-in.

Excitement was through the roof.

The track trumpet blared, signaling the start of the seventh race. The announcer's voice rang through the loudspeakers: "The horses are on the track!"

Game on.

The Race

Sols Venture was led to the starting gate.

He settled in.

Then—BANG!

The bell rang. The gates flew open.

They were off!

Sols broke fast, taking third place right out of the gate. It was a short race, just six furlongs.

That's about a minute and twelve seconds from start to finish.

No room for error.

The jockey, decked out in those crazy silks, wasted no time. He went to the whip, urging Sols forward.

It worked. Sols kept coming. Now he was in second.

By this point, we were losing our minds.

The baseball manager was screaming louder than any of us.

Then it happened.

Sols Venture made his move. He surged forward, passing the horse in first place.

As he edged ahead, he grazed the other horse ever so slightly.

No big deal.

Then the track announcer's voice boomed through the speakers: "AT THE WIRE IT'S SOLS VENTURE!"

We lost it.

SOL'S VENTURE FUCKING WON!

The restaurant erupted. We were hugging, kissing, cheering. It was pure, unfiltered joy.

It was a massive payday.

My uncle ordered champagne for the entire restaurant. Within minutes, bottles were popping as I ran down to the winner's circle with my cousins.

We lined up for the official winner's photo—my father, Ben, the trainer, my cousins, and of course, the star of the hour Sols Venture.

The photographer snapped the picture.

It was perfect.

Then a flashing light caught my eye. I looked up at the tote board.

Sol's Venture's number was blinking. So was the second-place horse's number.

Inquiry.

For those unfamiliar with horse racing, an inquiry means a violation may have occurred, something that could change the official results of the race.

Our celebration came to a screeching halt.

The Decision

The track stewards' job is to review each race and ensure there are no violations.

Well, remember when Sols Venture went to pass the leader and barely grazed the other horse as he surged ahead?

That was the violation in question.

We sat there, waiting. Three minutes stretched into what felt like a fucking lifetime.

We had already mentally counted our winnings.

Then, just like that the verdict was in.

They ruled it was a violation. Sols Venture was taken down from first place to second.

He fucking lost.

One second, we were standing in the winner's circle, basking in glory. We had just taken the official winner's photo, frozen in time, proof that for one shining moment, we had won.

I still have that picture on my phone today.

But just like that...it was gone.

Same Old Story

Not long after, my father would lose the garment business due to his brother's shenanigans. Loyalty!

All the newfound wealth. Gone.

A few years later, they would all end up in jail. And eventually, they'd have to start over.

A recurring theme.

Second place.

The Wake-Up

Suddenly, I wake up.

I rub my eyes, blinking as the dream fades.

Outside my window, I see nothing but open fields.

Horses. Grazing.

And just like that, my mind drifts back to my dream...A Day at the Races.

7

Deer Hunter

I wake up from a nap that feels like two hours, but in reality, it was only twenty minutes. Still, I feel refreshed, and the sadness I was carrying before has lightened. This entire trip has been an emotional roller coaster—up, down, side to side. One minute I'm laughing; the next I'm drowning in sorrow.

My brother is driving, and for some reason, Cousin is messing with the GPS, claiming he's trying to find a faster route. It's a miracle we're still heading in the right direction. I'm half-expecting to wake up and find us in Upstate New York. But my brother figures as long as we stick to Route 80, we'll be fine. So, all is good. Lewisburg is about fifty miles away, roughly an hour to go.

A Hunter's Guide

Cousin keeps going on about how much he loves Pennsylvania. I turn to him and say, "What the fuck do you know about Pennsylvania?"

He grins. "Michael, I used to come here all the time with our older cousin, Nicky. We went deer hunting."

My brother raises an eyebrow. "Really? I never knew you guys went hunting."

Cousin puffs up his chest. "Hell yeah. We shot rabbits, deer and sometimes even ducks."

At first, I think he's full of shit. But then he starts laying out the rules—licensing, hunting seasons, the whole protocol. He explains how you have to tag the animal properly, how you transport it afterward strapped to the grill of a car or truck like some trophy.

Alright, maybe this guy really did go deer hunting.

The next logical question, "You ever actually shoot a deer?"

Cousin doesn't miss a beat. "Hell yeah! Every time I did, it was better than sex."

He goes on about how he'd sit up in a tree for hours, camouflaged, in the dead of winter. His only source of warmth was cheap whiskey from a flask. Sometimes, he'd wait for hours before he could "get off a shot." Most times he missed and came home empty-handed.

I blink. "And that's fun?"

My brother and I never had the urge to go out and kill something for sport. It just didn't appeal to us. What's the thrill in that?

But hey, if that's what he enjoys, all power to him. I'm not here to judge. Whatever floats your boat.

Cousin then starts listing off the different rifles he owns, the fancy scopes he uses. I shake my head.

"The difference between you and me," I tell him, "is you need a gun and all your fancy scopes to kill a deer. You gotta sit in the freezing cold for hours, waiting."

Cousin fires back, "Yeah? And you never shot shit. How the fuck else you gonna kill a deer—what, with your cock?"

My brother bursts out laughing. He looks at me, and I smirk.

"Sit back," I say. "I got a story for you."

Because in life, some stories fade away.

And others? They stay with you forever.

Story Time Begins

"Cousin, it starts with David and me on a road trip to pick up my father after his jail sentence was completed. He had been 'doing a bid' again—this time in Pennsylvania—at the Federal Correctional Institution in Loretto. He had just finished an eighteen-month stretch, and we were making the trip to bring him home. Now, Loretto is a hell of a lot farther than Lewisburg, so a little planning was involved. He was scheduled to be released at six in the morning, which meant we had to leave the night before and crash at a local motel. The plan was simple. Get there late, grab a few hours of sleep, and wake up early so we'd be at the prison by 5:30 a.m. But...there's a caveat to this story."

Cousin interrupts. "What are you speaking French now? What the fuck is 'caveat'?"

I laugh. "Dopey, it means like a special situation, a certain condition. Ok, can I fucking continue?"

Cousin quietly answered, "Yeah go ahead. Einstein."

I continue.

"Here's the thing. We had a guest on this trip. Some guy my father had befriended while doing his bid at Loretto. This guy had been released four months earlier, and my father insisted he come along for the ride. We'd never met him before. The plan was for him to meet us at our house in Corona."

I continued. "So, we're outside waiting for this guy, and after about half an hour, he finally pulls up in a brand new 1983 Dodge Aries K. The car was the new model at the time, a beautiful baby-blue, four-door sedan with a light grey leather interior. How did we know it was brand new?"

"The goddamn sales sticker was still on the side window."

"He steps out, introduces himself, and off we go. His name was Danny, and he was massive. Had to be at least six-foot-seven and pushing three-hundred-fifty pounds. The guy looked like he could've been an offensive tackle for the Giants."

"Am I right, Dave?" I ask.

My brother just shakes his head and laughs. "Absolutely. Fucking guy was a mountain."

"Now, as you know, Cousin, on long trips like this, we take turns driving. Danny took the first shift, so we headed out, crossing the Whitestone Bridge."

"It's the middle of July, around four in the afternoon, and while we're driving, Danny starts talking about his time with my father inside. He's going on about how much he respects him, how he'd do anything for him. That kind of shit."

"Guys like Danny? While they're locked up, they like to befriend people with so-called 'influence.' It makes them feel safe. Gives them protection."

"At this point, the conversation is still light, just getting to know each other, making small talk. I say, 'Hey Danny, nice car.'"

"He grins, clearly excited about it. He had just picked it up that same day and was itching to see what it could do on the highway."

"As we drive, the conversation shifts to baseball—the Yankees, Billy Martin, and how many times the guy got fired and rehired. Meanwhile, Danny starts leaning on the gas pedal, testing out his new toy."

"He's loving it. Sure, the car isn't a Corvette, but he's happy. It's got a smooth ride. No traffic, clear roads."

"After about three hours, we decide to grab some dinner. We've just crossed into Pennsylvania, but we've still got another three hours to go."

Another Diner, Another Meal

"We found another quiet town with a small diner and grabbed some dinner. Like I mentioned earlier, all these diners in small towns had that same throwback look—unchanged for decades. Simple. No frills. Just good comfort food."

"It was a little awkward for us because, well, we didn't know this fucking guy. But in life, sometimes you just roll with the punches."

"Now, Cuz, do you know what that means? Einstein?" I ask.

He shoots me a look and, under his breath, mutters with a smirk, "Go fuck yourself. Sarcastic prick."

I took that as confirmation he understood and continued.

"We ordered our food, and this monster ordered damn near the entire left side of the menu. I'm not kidding. The guy ate like he was going to the chair."

"After we finished, he motioned to the waitress for the check. 'It's on me, fellas,' he said."

"We tried to pay, but he wasn't having it. As we got up to leave, I turned to Danny. 'Take a break from driving, I got it.'"

"Danny nodded and said, 'Sounds good. I'm a little tired.' He tossed me the keys. I slid into the driver's seat, Danny took the passenger side, and Dave jumped in the back. And this is where the story gets interesting..."

Back on the Road

"I settled into the driver's seat, adjusted the mirrors, and got ready to roll. Dave sat in the back with the map open, navigating."

"This was 1983. No GPS. We had to make sure we got on Route I-76, the Pennsylvania Turnpike. We still had a long drive ahead, but after a solid meal, I had the energy to go for hours. I was twenty years old and full of piss and vinegar. Glancing at the gas gauge, I saw we were at half a tank."

"I turned to Danny. 'Maybe we should fill up now. That way, in the morning, we can just get up and go pick up my father. It's gonna be a bitch finding a gas station at 5:30 a.m.'"

"Danny agreed. On our way to the Turnpike, we spotted a station and pulled in. I rolled down the window. 'Fill it up.'"

"Danny reached into his pocket. 'I got it.'"

"Out of respect for my father, he wasn't letting us pay for anything. Cuz, you know how that shit works."

"The attendant not only filled the tank but also wiped down the windshield and back window—bugs splattered everywhere from driving through a hot summer night. The car had a fresh wax job that made the baby-blue paint pop."

"Even the gas station attendant noticed. 'Man, I had to clean these windows. This car is way too shiny to be covered in bugs.'"

"I thanked him, Danny paid for the gas, and even threw in a generous tip. Nice touch."

"Now, all I had to do was find the Turnpike, navigate the side streets, and follow the signs."

Keep Both Hands on the Wheel

"I merged onto the Turnpike, keeping it steady. The speed limit was 65, but I wanted to test the engine a little. I pushed it up to seventy-five, and it handled smooth as hell."

Cousin hollers from the back. "Seventy-five?! That's it?! You fucking pussy!"

I laugh. "Cousin, calm the fuck down and let me finish the story."

"Meanwhile, Danny started telling us about his life. He was from Staten Island and owned a construction company. Just idle conversation, passing time. Within an hour, both Danny and Dave knocked out, leaving me alone with the radio."

"Now, remember that this was 1983. No preset stations. No internet radio. Just me, blindly searching for something decent to listen to."

"First, I hit three Christian stations. Nope."

"Then, a few country stations. Fuck no."

"Finally I struck gold. A rock station. Good music? I could drive all night."

Dave mumbles from the back, "There was no sports radio back then. Just music."

Cousin groans. "How the fuck did we survive?"

A Song, Then Death on the Turnpike

"I remember this like it was yesterday. I'm cruising in the left lane at seventy-five miles an hour. It's about ten minutes to nine on a warm July night, and we're just about to lose the last bit of sunlight."

"The radio is on, and Fleetwood Mac's "Tusk" is playing. Great song. I'm into it, singing along 'Just tell me that you want me...TUSK!'"

"The song has this incredible horn section, and I'm motioning like I'm playing the horns while driving."

"And then BANG!"

"A fucking deer, out of nowhere, charges onto the Turnpike. This cocksucker jumps straight in front of the car."

"Remember, I'm in the left lane doing seventy-five. There's zero time to react. No braking. Nothing. The only brake was the impact itself."

Cousin yells, "HOLY SHIT!"

"Cousin, after hitting the deer, Dave and Danny bolt awake. Danny said, 'WHAT THE FUCK?!'"

"I can still hear the sound. The deer slamming into the grill, bones crunching like snapping twigs. And this wasn't some little Bambi-looking deer. This was a big motherfucker. Horns and all."

Cousin yells, "It's called a rack, you dumb fuck!"

I shot back, "Yeah, whatever. Probably bigger than anything you ever shot, Bungalow Bill."

"For three solid seconds, this thing is embedded in the grill. Then, like a goddamn movie, it flips up and smashes into the windshield. CRACK."

"The Aries K swerves all over the Turnpike. It's a miracle I don't flip this car or send us crashing into a ditch."

"Finally, the deer flies over the windshield, slams against the roof, and disappears behind us. The whole thing lasted maybe ten seconds. But it felt like a lifetime."

Cousin is on the edge of his seat. "What the fuck happened next?!"

"I pulled over, still stunned. My brain isn't even processing that we just barely escaped death. All I can think about?"

"Danny's BRAND-NEW CAR. The fucking sales sticker was still on the window."

"I sat there, frozen, afraid to get out and look at the damage."

"But we finally step outside, and the first thing we see? Deer fur floating up from the grill and radiator. The front of the car? Fucking demolished."

"The windshield? Cracked to shit. And the worst part?"

"We just had the damn thing cleaned."

Cousin turns to Dave. "Is this true?"

Dave still laughing, "Yep. Every word."

"WOW," Cousin replied.

Bedtime

"Cousin, I must have apologized a thousand times to Danny. To his credit, he took it like a champ."

"There was nothing you could've done," Danny said. "The cocksucker jumped out of nowhere. Don't worry. It's just a car. It can be fixed. Thank God you kept it under control."

"At least he wasn't pissed. But I still felt horrible. This guy was a stranger. W had met him just hours ago."

"Now? I wrecked his brand-new car."

"We climbed back inside, praying the car was still drivable. After a few turns of the key, thank God it started. Danny took the wheel this time. I moved to the passenger seat, still feeling like absolute shit."

"At this point, we just wanted to get through the night and get my father home. About a half-hour later, we reached the motel, a single room, two queen beds. One bed for me and Dave. One for Danny."

"And let me tell you, my adrenaline was still pumping."

"I kept envisioning this giant motherfucker killing me in my sleep. So, yeah. Uncomfortable night, to say the least."

Early Morning Release

"We were up at 4:30 a.m., took quick showers, and were out the door. I just wanted to pick up my father, get back to New York, and never see Danny again."

"To his credit, he kept reassuring me. 'No worries, not your fault.'"

"But I still felt like shit, especially knowing how much he loved that car."

"Loretto Penitentiary was only a half-hour from the motel. Once again, I found myself praying (did a lot of praying on this trip) that the car would start and actually get us back to New York. When we arrived, we made a group decision: Do NOT tell my father what happened until we were safely back in New York."

Cousin asks, "How the hell were you planning to hide the wrecked car from your father?"

I smirk. "Easy. We parked with the BACK of the car facing the facility. When he comes out, he goes straight to the back seat. He won't see the front damage. As for the windshield? We'll just say a rock from the road hit it."

Can We Please Just Get Back to New York?

"Just as planned, my father walked out of Loretto Penitentiary at 6:00 a.m. sharp. We got out of the car to greet him. Hugs, kisses, the whole nine yards. Then, we immediately steered him toward the back seat."

"At first, he wanted to sit up front. No fucking way. We insisted he'd be more comfortable in the back. Thank God he agreed. He slid in next to Dave, and off we went, headed straight for New York City."

"The plan was to go to the garment center and meet up with some friends. Meanwhile, I spent the entire ride gripping the passenger seat, holding my breath. I kept waiting for the radiator to blow and leave us stranded in the middle of Pennsylvania."

"I can't even recall what we talked about during that drive. Today, it's all a blur."

"What I *do* remember, though? Passing the exact spot where I hit the deer."

"We were now cruising I-76 East, but the night before, I had been officially christened as a "Deer Hunter" while driving I-76 West. And wouldn't you fucking know it?"

"As we drove past, we saw that same damn deer lying on the side of the road."

"I just put my head down. I didn't look. I didn't want to see it. I just wanted to see the sign that said NEW YORK."

"We didn't even stop. Not just because we were afraid my father would notice the car's condition, but because we were terrified that if we turned the car off, it might not start again."

"Hours later, we finally pulled into the garment district in Manhattan. And all I felt was relief. At that point, I could give a fuck. We were home. The car made it."

"We pulled into an indoor garage, shut off the engine. BOOM. The radiator blew."

"I just cringed. And that's when we finally told my father what happened."

Cousin asks, "What did he say?"

I shrug. "Danny, sorry about your car. I'm hoping your insurance covers this? I mean what else could he say?"

See Ya

"I remember shaking Danny's hand and saying, 'Hey, pleasure meeting you. Hope to see you soon!'"

"I knew that was bullshit. I was well aware I'd probably never see this guy again."

"And as events unfolded? I was right. It was a wild, unforgettable moment in time with a guy I knew for all of twenty-four hours."

"Months later, I finally asked my father what happened to Danny."

He shrugged. "I saw him maybe once again, and that was it."

"That poor bastard won't forget us, though."

"Oh, and the car? Yeah... totaled. Oh well."

Claim of Victory

"Cousin, so you can take your rifles, your scopes, and your fancy-ass hunting permits and shove them up your ass!"

For the first and probably last time, Cousin had nothing to say. Because at that moment, he knew...

I was the ultimate Deer Hunter.

8

Going to California

Sing Along

Picture this. I'm a kid sitting in front of the TV and hear a song fill my living room. "Well, the first thing you know ole Jed's a millionaire."

Who's Jed? My eyes wide.

Next the TV sang, "Jed move away from there. Californy is the place you ought to be."

California? As a kid from Queens, I was intrigued. What the hell did I know about California?

"They loaded up the truck and they moved to Beverly."

To me it was just some far-off, sunny place where movies were made and it never rained.

"Hills that is…swimming pools, movie stars."

I was hooked.

If you're old enough, you'll recognize those lyrics from the theme song of a popular 1960s TV show *The Beverly Hillbillies.*

The show followed a family from the deep South who accidentally struck oil, became instant millionaires, and moved to Beverly Hills, California. It was hilarious, and I loved it.

That show brought California into my home every Wednesday night. And when it eventually went into syndication, I watched it whenever it came on.

Fast-forward a few years—1978, to be exact—and suddenly, California wasn't just some TV fantasy anymore.

It became a place I'd visit often.

On the Road Again

We'd been on this road trip for just over four hours when we decided to pull over one last time.

The clock on the dash of my SUV read 11:03 a.m., and according to the GPS, we still had about thirty miles to go, which meant, barring traffic, we were about thirty-five minutes from the penitentiary.

Yesterday while talking to Warden Scurti, he told me that my father's body wouldn't be available for viewing until 1:00 p.m. That meant we had at least two hours before the guards would let us in.

I figured leaving early would give us some cushion time in case of traffic, but the roads had been clear. Now we had plenty of time to kill.

A Quick Pit Stop

As we pulled off the highway, we spotted a huge sign: HANK'S SPORTS BAR →

Dave pointed it out. "Let's hit the sports bar. We can watch ESPN, check the scores, maybe grab a beer."

Cousin immediately perked up. "Good idea. I had a bet on the Yankees last night, and I haven't checked the score yet."

Now, let me explain. Cousin was a degenerate gambler.

This guy would put money on two cockroaches racing if given the chance.

I thought, *Beer at 11 a.m.? A little early...No?*

But after four hours of nothing but small-town diners, a sports bar sounded like a solid change of scenery. "Fuck it. Let's go."

We followed the signs for about two miles before spotting a big neon sign: HANK'S SPORTS BAR – OPENS AT 11 AM

Perfect.

I figured we could kill an hour-and-a-half and still have plenty of time to get to Lewisburg.

The parking lot was empty, and we walked inside.

Inside Hank's

The place was decked out in sports memorabilia. Autographed baseballs, basketballs, framed jerseys, and photos—all dedicated to Philadelphia sports.

Not my cup of tea, but I had to admit it was a cool setup.

Since it was just after opening, the place was completely empty. We grabbed seats at the bar, where they had three massive TVs mounted above.

Immediately, the smell of stale beer from the previous night's crowd of thirsty Philly fans hit me.

Each TV had something different on:

Left screen: SportsCenter
Center screen: Some European soccer match
Right screen: ESPN Classic

I plopped down in front of the ESPN Classic screen.

The bartender, a guy named John, came over and introduced himself. We ordered three Heinekens on tap, and within two minutes, he placed frosted mugs in front of us.

Ice-cold. Delicious.

Cousin checked his Yankees score.

Wouldn't you know it? He fucking won.

He was grinning ear to ear, happy as a pig in shit.

He slammed his fist on the bar and shouted, "BEERS ON ME!"

A Blast from the Past

On ESPN Classic, they were replaying Game Six of the 1978 World Series—my favorite.

Yankees vs. Dodgers.

Yankees won that series in six games, clinching yet another World Series title, their twenty-second, but who's counting?

The game was played in Dodger Stadium in Los Angeles, California.

And just like that, watching that game took me back in time.

I was right back in California.

I started thinking about how, back in the day, my father and his business partner, Ben, had two beautiful apartments in Hollywood.

My father's place was on the ninth floor, with a huge balcony that overlooked Century City.

That area was a major business hub with great restaurants, high-end shopping, and all the glitz and glamor California was known for.

I remembered visiting him, sitting out on that balcony.

In the mornings, the city was covered in fog/smog, making it impossible to see much.

But within a few hours, the warm California sun would burn through the haze, revealing the palm trees, the skyscrapers, and the distant mountains.

It was breathtaking.

And at night? Forget it. The lights, the skyline, the energy of the city—it was like another world.

A long, long way from Queens.

You're probably wondering *How the hell did a kid from Queens end up in Hollywood, California?*

Well...

Let me tell you.

California Dreaming

The year was 1978. I was sixteen years old, a junior in high school, and my father was at the peak of his success.

This was before he went to prison.

He was resilient, and he always found a way to bounce back. But he would never reach the heights of 1978 again.

He had successful pizzerias, was killing it in the rag business, had a stake in thoroughbred horses, and, of course, various "street undertakings".

I live by an unwritten code, so I don't need to define what those street ventures were. I'll just leave it to your imagination.

It works better that way. Am I right?

But just so we're clear: IT HAD NOTHING TO DO WITH DRUGS.

My father never touched that business. He thought it was dirty, not something he wanted any part of. He wasn't about that.

He always said, "There are other ways to skin the cat."

There was big money in drugs, sure.

But money was never my father's God.

Intoxicating & Fascinating

I remember cutting school early and heading into the city to work at his company Classic Fit.

The experience was unmatched. The people I met—characters from all walks of life—were one-of-a-kind.

Like I said before, working in the pizzerias gave me Ivy League smarts.

But working in the garment center? That was graduate school.

It was just another level.

At that point, my mother's influence on education was starting to fade into the background. It was hard not to get swept up in all the flash and excitement.

I started thinking, *Who the hell needs school? I can just jump into all these businesses.*

The whole lifestyle was intoxicating.

I was barely scraping by in school, doing just enough to keep my mother off my back. But deep down, I already knew I was done with school.

And it broke my mother's heart.

That world—the thrill, the fast money, the power—was like a beautiful woman or a dangerous drug. I had gone off the rails a little.

But eventually, I learned if you keep your eyes and ears open, life will teach you things that no school ever could. We'll get to that...

Fashion & Music

By the late seventies, designer jeans had taken over fashion. A few years earlier, denim jeans were just "dungarees", and everyone wore them. Dungaree jackets. Overalls. Wrangler, Lee, Levi's, Big Smiths—all the old-school brands.

But suddenly?

The big designer names came in and wiped them out.

At Classic Fit, we designed women's budget blouses, so why the hell were crates of designer jeans being shipped to our warehouse?

I had no idea. All I knew was that I was signing off on boxes and boxes of them.

And it wasn't just jeans.

We were also getting tons of record albums, the hottest ones of the time.

The disco craze was at its peak, and one movie had defined the movement, a box office smash. I can't tell you how many cases of that soundtrack album I opened and stacked in our shipping department.

And it wasn't just that one. We had all the top artists of the time, albums filling box after box.

I had no clue why we were receiving all this stuff. But I did know one thing: The return address on every shipping label said LOS ANGELES, CALIFORNIA.

A Star Is Born

Turns out, my father and his business partner, Ben, had somehow taken over a company in California that produced all this merchandise.

That meant they were constantly flying back and forth between New York and California.

And whenever I was off from school? I was on a 747 jet straight to LAX.

I had no idea what the backstory of this company was. All I knew was that it was raining money.

The company cars? Jaguars. Mercedes-Benzes. A Cadillac limousine with a private driver.

For a kid from Queens, this was fantasyland.

Every time I landed in L.A., it felt like Disneyland™.

I remember sitting in the back of the limo, looking out the window. People—young kids, girls, tourists—would wave at me, thinking I must have been someone famous.

At first, I just stared, confused.

Until Ben leaned over and said, "Just wave back."

So I did. On command.

Like a pro.

And at that moment, I wasn't thinking about school. I wasn't worried about geometry or trigonometry. Can you blame me?

The Transformation

Soon my wardrobe changed. I traded in my dungarees for designer jeans.

My father bought me a diamond initial pinky ring. A diamond watch. And a custom-made pendant for me and my siblings with our birth dates in diamonds.

Mine?

"12/22" in all diamonds. And I still have that pendant forty-six years later.

I was in love with California.

Back at Hank's

Hank's was starting to fill up with its regulars, and soon there wasn't a single empty seat at the bar.

Right on cue, Reggie Jackson smacked another home run, and the Philly faithful in the bar started chirping. They were yelling what Reggie was famous for saying, "Mr. October! The straw that stirs the drink!"

(For all you youngsters: When Reggie Jackson signed with the Yankees in 1977, he declared himself the new leader of the team. Hence, the legendary "straw that stirs the drink" line.)

Cousin motioned to John, the bartender. "John, three more Heinekens."

I wasn't really feeling another beer because I was driving, and the thought of state troopers was still fresh in my mind. I shook my head. "No, I'm good."

But Cousin wasn't having it. "C'mon, have one for our guy Reggie!"

Well...I folded like a cheap suit. "John, put 'em in frosted mugs."

Peer pressure.

John nodded, and out came three more ice-cold beers.

Cousin sat there grinning ear to ear.

Back in My Time Machine

I remember the pure exhilaration of going to California.

Queens felt like I was living life in black and white; while California was like stepping into Technicolor™.

Let me paint you a picture...Close your eyes and picture that scene in *The Wizard of Oz*.

Dorothy's house crashes down. She opens the door, and BOOM—black and white turns into the beautiful, colorful Land of Oz.

That was exactly how I felt.

This kid from Queens was officially living the life.

The Adventure

One of the best parts of going to California was the plane ride.

It was a six-hour flight, but we'd kill time telling stories and laughing the whole way to LAX.

I still remember my first trip.

I was traveling with my father, Ben, his two kids, and Grace.

My father and Ben were up in first class, while Grace and I were right behind them, first row in coach.

As I've said before, Grace and I are kindred spirits. We share the same values, the same sense of humor.

For six straight hours, I kept her entertained by telling her stories (mostly about Diamond, because trust me, there were many).

Every story started the same way, "Wow, do I have a story to tell you."

And Grace? She laughed at everything.

I always loved that about her.

The Set Up

One story I vividly remember telling her was about growing up in Corona.

She already knew The Tape Story, as did the entire neighborhood.

But this one? This was about psycho Nino, my friend Sal, and yours truly.

Now, my buddy Sal lived on my block. He was first-generation Italian, and his parents were quiet, polite people—immigrants who came to the U.S. in the late fifties. They spoke with heavy accents and kept to themselves.

Sal was one of the six guys in our crew, the one who was always high. This kid smoked more weed than Cheech and Chong.

(For those who don't know, Cheech and Chong were famous comedic actors in the seventies who made movies glorifying the beauty of pot smoking.)

Grace already knew Nino and Sal, so she was eager to hear another story.

Story Time

Sal and I were best friends, and we had just met two girls from the neighborhood park. Before long, they became our girlfriends. We were all thirteen.

Our first girlfriends.

We were in heaven, spending every waking second with them.

I was like a kid who discovered candy for the first time and couldn't stay away from the candy store. If you catch my drift. Life was coming at me fast, and I was devouring it.

The girls were also best friends and lived right across the street from each other.

It was the perfect setup.

So where does Nino fit into all this? Well, as I've mentioned before our whole crew lived on the same block. And we were always up to hijinks.

Nino and I? We took great joy in messing with Sal's parents.

They were nice, wonderful, quiet people.

And we were just being…little assholes.

A Work of Art

You know when you're taking a hot shower, the steam fogs up the mirror and you can write or draw on the glass?

Well, on humid New York summer nights, the same thing happened to car windows.

So, naturally we decorated the windows of Sal's father's car. And when I say decorated…I mean we drew the most detailed, graphic, pornographic images you can imagine.

And Nino? This kid was like a fucking Picasso.

(Thanks to his massive collection of nudie magazines, his artistic skills were advanced.)

This went on all summer.

And Sal? Clueless.

Life Was Coming Fast

"So, Grace, one night, me, Sal, and our girlfriends were drinking beer in the park, and let's just say we were all feeling no pain."

"We decided to head back to Sal's girlfriend's house, but since her parents were home, we stayed outside just hanging around the block. There were some other kids around, so someone suggested, 'Let's play tag.'"

"Tag. Drunken tag."

At this point, Grace interrupted. "What time was this?"

"Had to be around ten o'clock. It was pitch black."

I continued, "So we're running around like drunken maniacs, when suddenly Sal trips, smashes to the ground, and cracks his head on the concrete."

"I ran over, and he was laughing his ass off. But his face was covered in blood."

"Sal, you crazy fuck, you're bleeding like a sieve!"

"Right then, his girlfriend's parents came running over. Keep in mind we were plastered, but we had to play sober."

"They brought Sal inside to check his injury. The cut was right above his left eyebrow. After about five minutes, the bleeding wouldn't stop."

"So they told him, 'Sal, you need stitches. Call your parents. You gotta go to the hospital.'"

"Sal hesitated for a second then called his father. Within ten minutes, his parents arrived."

A Long Car Ride

"Sal's mom and dad were sitting up front. His little sister was in the backseat. Sal jumped in, and I held my breath."

"I was praying his parents wouldn't smell the beer on him. If they found out we were drinking? They'd go straight to Mommy and that wouldn't be good."

"I spent the whole night worrying. Did they know? Was I fucked?"

"The next morning, I was dying to see Sal. But I wouldn't dare go to his house, not until I knew if his parents were onto us. So I went straight to the park, where Nino and the rest of our psychotic friends were hanging out."

"Around 11 a.m. Sal finally showed up wearing a huge bandage over his eye."

"I looked at him. 'Sal, what the fuck happened?'"

"Sal glared at me. 'YOU FUCKING GUYS! NINO, YOU COCKSUCKER!'"

"We played dumb. 'What? What are you talking about?'"

An Unexpected Peep Show

"Apparently, it had been hot and muggy the night before. And on the way to the hospital, the windows fogged up. And yes, you guessed it."

"Right in front of his entire family's eyes, penises. Vaginas. Everywhere. A fucking masterpiece."

"Imagine this: His mother and little sister were in the car and suddenly, in the dim glow of the streetlights, the artwork on the windows appeared in full display. Sal's father, in his thick Italian accent, turned to him. 'Sal... whatta friends a doin' to me?!'"

"We couldn't hold back. We were dying laughing."

"Sal? Not so much."

The Aftermath

"His mother had a different reaction. She went straight to Nino's house and told his mom. Grace, not our house. Just Nino's. Fucking Nino took all the hits."

"And remember what his crazy Sicilian mother did to him over The Tape incident?"

"Well, guess what? She did it again. Out came the scissors and Nino came out of that house looking like a lawnmower ran over his head. Meanwhile, I skated one more time."

Fasten Seat Belts. Time to Land.

Grace was laughing uncontrollably. Passengers on the plane—reading, napping, trying to relax—kept shushing her.

Looking back, it was a time when life was simple. Innocent. Easy.

I guess as we get older, things get more complicated. But man, I miss the good old days.

Don't you?

As the plane descended, the view was incredible. The sun was setting, casting a golden glow over the mountains, palm trees, and the city lights below.

For once, Grace and I didn't say a word. We just sat there captivated by California.

Good Day Sunshine

By morning, we headed out early to visit Ben and my father's new business, the same place that had been shipping all those boxes I had opened back in New York.

I had been expecting something big. Something flashy. Something that made sense.

Instead just a random building in an industrial park.

Nondescript. No fancy sign. No offices.

Nothing.

I stood there, staring at it, thinking *What the fuck?*

But I didn't ask any questions. We stayed maybe five minutes, then got right back in the limo and headed to the Santa Anita racetrack.

It was a perfect California day. Sunshine. Warm air. No New York humidity.

There's an old song from the early seventies that perfectly describes California, "It Never Rains in Southern California" by Albert Hammond.

And let me tell you that fucking guy was spot on. Every damn day was better than the last.

You gotta love this place.

Betting on the Ponies

It wasn't long before we found ourselves having another Day at the Races.

Not long after our Sols Venture disaster back in New York, we were back in the game—this time at Santa Anita, one of the most beautiful racetracks in the country.

The place was stunning.

We grabbed a table at the track's restaurant and started touting horses, betting lingo for doing research. That's when we found him, a horse named Humble Howard.

I'll never forget him.

He wasn't like any horse I had ever seen—a light gray, almost white, absolutely stood out from the field.

And his name? Perfect.

We didn't bother touting this race. We just bet it all on Humble Howard. It's funny the things you remember.

The horses were in the gate. The bell rang and they were off!

And Humble Howard? He broke late.

By the first turn? Dead last.

Field of eight. He was eighth.

For most of the race, he just stayed there, dragging behind, looking like a long shot at best.

Then the final turn. The jockey went to the whip and Humble Howard took off like he had a rocket up his ass! Somehow, the entire field opened up right in front of him.

Like Moses parting the Red Sea.

You could have driven a truck through that opening. That beautiful white horse came flying down the middle of the track from dead last to first.

And won the race!

We went nuts, cashed in a few bucks, and had the time of our lives.

Life was coming fast. I was sixteen, going on forty-six.

Glory Days

California was a time in our lives that my father never duplicated again. It turned out to be the pinnacle before the fall.

For years, he leaned on this time, these memories—almost like a self-medicating thought process.

It was his way of getting through the tougher times.

People do that, don't they? I know I do.

They go back to better days, replaying them over and over to dull the pain of the present. Like the high school jock who never moved past his glory days.
1978?

That was my father's glory year.

A financial windfall.

A roller coaster ride at Coney Island—fast, thrilling, and unforgettable.

Parting Shot

But with every downfall, there are lessons learned.

And do you know what 1978 taught me? You can have it all...you just can't have it all at once.

Patience, my friends.

Oh, and if you're wondering what was really going on with that California business? Rumor has it that they were bootlegging designer jeans and albums and selling them to vendors.

I was just a kid, what the hell did I know?

But if you guessed that before I told you, congratulations. You win the golden ticket.

The clock on the wall at Hank's read 12:10 p.m., and we still had time to kill before heading to Lewisburg.

But this time I had a pit in my stomach because I knew what was ahead.

And I knew that this time I wasn't Going to California.

9

Tipping Point

I just finished my Heineken as I watched the Yankees celebrate their 1978 World Series victory on the field. My emotions were bittersweet. The series was over, but for me, it marked the end of the euphoric tidal wave of my father's success. It was a two-year meteoric climb from a blue-collar grind to an opulent lifestyle that, looking back, felt like it had been running on borrowed time.

At the time, I was working long, brutal hours at the pizzerias, while Diamond was knocking out people left and right. The air was thick with flour and sweat, the relentless rhythm of dough-stretching and sauce-spreading ingrained in my muscle memory.

I can still recall the flour under my fingernails and the smell of it on my clothes. I smelled like work.

And then, just like that, my nails were manicured, and my body was drenched in cologne. Once, sometimes twice a week, my father, his crew, my brother, and I would head to Pipo of Rome in Manhattan, a high-end men's salon in the heart of the garment district.

This was no barbershop with the candy-striped pole out front!

That's for damn sure.

At sixteen, I was handed the keys to a brand-new Cadillac Coupe DeVille. I was drowning—no, marinating—in a lifestyle no teenage kid should be living. But then again, what the hell is *normal?*

The allure of it all was intoxicating. Money, power, status—they seduced me like a beautiful woman whispering sweet nothings in my ear. And before I knew it, I was hooked.

Unfortunately, the lure got me.

Back then, I didn't have the wisdom to understand that success built on quicksand doesn't last. I didn't see the cracks forming beneath my feet. I had no reason to question it.

Who the fuck would have known?

I measured people by their bank accounts, judged them by the cars they drove, the suits they wore. That's how I was wired back then.

You might be wondering, *How do you come back from that?*

Quiet Time at Hank's

My cousin leaned over, tapped me on the shoulder, and asked with a smirk, "Michael, you cool?"

I nodded. "Yeah, all good. Just thinking about my father."

He chuckled. "How much time we got till we head to Lewisburg?"

"About half an hour."

He whispered, "Good, I gotta hit the john and drop a deuce."

I laughed. "Go enjoy."

With that, he shot off toward the men's room.

Dave and I, still sitting at the bar, exchanged knowing smiles. My older brother, my partner in survival, had lived every single one of these experiences alongside me and our sister.

Shared experiences, different perspectives, and plenty of life lessons.

John the bartender strolled over. "Two more beers?"

We shook our heads. "You got a fresh pot of decaf?"

John frowned. "No, but I'll make one."

Dave nodded. "Appreciate it. Two cups, milk, no sugar."

As we sipped our coffee, we started swapping war stories, revisiting a past that felt both distant and all too familiar.

Grateful

Somehow, despite all the chaos, Dave, Grace, and I managed to carve out stable, successful lives. And by success, I don't just mean financial stability.

We took our beatings, earned our scars, and came out the other side wiser, tougher. Those bruises? They were lessons. Life's way of shaping us, molding us, forcing us to see the world as it truly is.

Pain and heartache have a funny way of steering you onto a different path, one you might never have chosen but one that ultimately leads to something real.

Today, success isn't just about money. It's about raising responsible kids who care about something bigger than themselves. It's about building a stable home, putting in the work, and reaping the rewards of effort and intention.

With all the madness, I still consider myself lucky.

I was raised by a strong, independent mother who kept us grounded, even when life was anything but. My father? He taught me to take risks, to believe that anything is possible.

And along the way, I had people who influenced me, shaped me, and became part of my foundation—part of my DNA.

I hit the lottery.

And no, it wasn't because of The Tape.

Love at First Sight

At eighteen, I met the future love of my life. She was in her senior year at Bayside High School, and I had graduated two years prior. For me, it was love at first sight. Some people say that kind of thing is a myth, but don't believe the skeptics.

She was seventeen and tall, slim, with beautiful dark brown hair and brown eyes. Stunning. I knew instantly that I would marry this girl. Earlier, I mentioned that if you're lucky, God brings you angels.

Well, she became the most important gift I would ever receive.

Her name is Antoinette, but we all called her Toni. She had, and still has, all the qualities I needed. She came from a big, loving Italian family—lots of aunts and uncles, that's for sure!

But for all their love, they didn't have a Diamond. He was with us.

Toni was fiercely independent, just like my mother. She was my mother 2.0.

Extremely intelligent, she graduated in the top fifteen of her high school class and later earned a master's degree in mathematics, building a successful career on Wall Street. Even today, when we go out with friends, she's still the prettiest woman in the room.

She is strong-willed and capable, the very things that drew me to her. Because of my mother's belief in me, I developed confidence and security, and an independent, strong woman wasn't a threat to me. In fact, it was an asset.

Meeting Toni was the first tipping point in my life. It changed everything.

It was the first step toward answering the question I posed earlier: *How do you come back from that?*

Change...Could Be a Good Thing

A tipping point is defined as the moment when a series of small changes become significant enough to cause a larger, *more important* change.

I believe every person experiences tipping point moments in life. The sad thing is some people don't recognize them until years later.

Ever hear someone say, "Wow, I should have never broken up with her. I was just young and stupid?"

Or, "Why didn't I listen to my parents? I regret not going to college."

Those were tipping points, moments that went ignored.

Sad.

I was lucky. I was intuitive enough to realize that Toni was my moment of change. And I've been holding on to that moment for forty-four years.

Back at the Bar

John came back with two fresh cups of coffee.

Dave said, "Thanks, John. And put the check on the guy who won the Yankee bet."

John laughed. "You got it."

I sat there, thinking about how my siblings and I evolved, how our lives could have taken drastically different paths.

I quietly said to Dave, "Looking back, I believe the moment that changed my life's path was when we were interviewed by the FBI. That was a tipping point in my life."

Dave raised an eyebrow. "Wow. The fucking FBI?"

He paused, then leaned in. "I'm curious. How so?"

His First "Pinch"

"Dave, I will take you back to that day. Not sure what you remember, but it was like I got hit with a lightning bolt! Do you remember the agent's name that came to see us?"

"Michael, sure I do. It was the first time we met Finnegan. He wound up following Daddy around for years after."

I smiled, "Yep, Agent Finnegan."

This was my father's first arrest, so the protocol prior to sentencing was new to us. Unfortunately, we all became veterans to the process years later.

Apparently, after the trial and prior to the judge's sentencing, an interview is scheduled. It's more like a testimony from family members. The purpose is to give the judge insight into the defendant who is about to be sentenced—the type of husband, father, and overall character. Family members hope all the nice things they say will result in a lenient decision. Not sure if it ever carries any weight, but it's a common protocol.

The FBI contacted my father's attorney and set up the date, time, and location of our choice. The agent was to interview my mom, Dave, and me. My sister was young at the time, so she skated. Lucky her!

We decided to have these so-called interviews at our home in Corona.

Wait, let's call it like it was—an *interrogation!*

I was nineteen at the time and nervous as hell. I mean, this was the FBI.

Hello, Mr. FBI

It was early October 1981, and Agent Finnegan arrived at our house around 7:00 in the evening. The plan was to interview us individually, which only made it more nerve-wracking.

In all fairness, Agent Finnegan seemed like a nice guy, just doing his job. A tall guy, about six-foot-three, thin, with a mustache. Dressed casually, but his clothes looked like they could have used a hot iron.

Pressed, he wasn't. That's for damn sure!

I still remember when he presented his badge. It was inside a small black wallet, worn and tattered.

Just like in the movies, he opened it and said, "Agent Finnegan, Federal Bureau of Investigation."

The sight of that badge made me realize Ok, this is legit!

Ranting and Venting

This was our first introduction to Finnegan. Over the years, he became a constant presence in our lives.

Not fun.

After a while, it just came with the territory. This is the side of the "glamorous lifestyle" that people don't see. They only know what they see in movies, on TV, or read in the papers. They only see the *glory*, but the *real* story? That would make them fucking run like they were competing in the hundred-yard dash at the Olympics™.

They have *no idea* what the constant presence of the FBI in your life is like.

The surprise visits. The waiting for the other shoe to drop. Not knowing what's coming next.

Phones being tapped.

That kind of shit.

Even though it was my father's life, don't think for a second that it didn't bleed onto his family. Then you meet people from the "Howdy Doody lifestyle," the ones who had uneventful, wholesome upbringings. These clowns walk around and act the part because they watched a few movies. We call them wannabes.

Or, to be blunt—*JERKOFFS!*

They have no clue what's behind the curtain. No *real* consequences.

And yet, they play their little act to impress their friends.

I gotta say—it gives me a good laugh.

And sometimes...It irritates me!

Ok, now that I got that off my chest.

Back to the Conversation with Dave

"Dave, I remember Mom's interview was first, you went second, and I was last. Dad and Mom were not on speaking terms at the time, and I was worried that she would not give a favorable interview."

Dave looked at me. "Shit, that's exactly what I was thinking."

"Dave, I said to myself, 'This is NOT going to be good for him.' Mom's interview lasted close to an hour while you and I were just sitting upstairs waiting to be called. Agent Finnegan then called your name and off you went."

"She came up and told me a little about what transpired, so I asked her about the types of questions and was cautiously feeling her out to see how she responded."

"She was a trooper and said, 'Michael, no matter how I feel about your father, I would never do anything to purposely hurt him, thus affecting you, Dave, and Grace.' Although she didn't approve, she held strong. Although she was angry, she didn't give up an inch!"

"Dave, she also went into detail about the agent's questions. For example, was he a loving and caring husband? Good father? That type of shit."

"She made him look like Ward Cleaver from *Leave it to Beaver*."
(For all you younglings, *Leave it to Beaver* was a 1950's TV show and Ward Cleaver was depicted as the quintessential dad. He even had the All-American name.)

I love my father, but believe me, he was no Ward Cleaver.

"About a half-hour later, you came up, and I was the next batter up. Dave, I remember. I quickly glanced over at you and tried to get a read by your body language of how it went."

"Your body spelled out one thing to me, and that was, R-E-L-I-E-F. So, you didn't give me much."

"I went down to the basement, and Agent Finnegan had this big notepad where he had taken notes. There were so many pages, I thought this fuck was writing *War and Peace*."

(Again, for all you post-boomers, *War and Peace* was a book of 1,200 pages.)

A lot of notes!

What the fuck!

"I went downstairs not knowing what to expect. I just knew I was to be respectful and courteous and try to be as helpful for my father as possible."

"Agent Finnegan stood up, shook my hand, showed me his badge, and started the 'interrogation'. Oops, I mean questions."

Side Bar

I was only nineteen years old and being questioned by the FBI. It was intimidating.

However, here is the flip-side.

I mentioned earlier that as a kid, none of my friends had a grandfather they called Diamond.

Cool, right?

Well, unlike me, my friends at nineteen weren't being questioned by the fucking FBI.

Not so cool anymore...

I repeatedly have said, my mother raised me with a sense of righteousness and taught me to hold myself to a high standard. I alluded to this earlier in the story regarding winding up in The Winners Circle. I didn't realize until this FBI moment how my self-worth would hit me right between the eyes.

Back to the Conversation with Dave

"So, Dave, the first questions were name, date of birth—just warm-up questions. I answered politely, then he started with probing questions regarding Daddy. His lifestyle? What did he do for a living? Did he live at home with us? What kind of man was he? It basically was a testimony on the type of father he was."

"Suddenly, I felt like I was being prosecuted! Now, I felt like I was in a vulnerable position and that I was being judged by a higher authority!"

"I felt this small." I held my thumb and forefinger, barely touching. "My emotions were raging, Who is this fucking guy to ask me these personal questions? He's a stranger!"

"At that moment, I said to myself, 'Hey, I'm better than this!' I felt being interrogated (yes, not questioned) was beneath me!"

"Not to sound arrogant, I believed I was raised to become the BEST version of myself."

NOT THIS.

I felt like *I WAS THE CRIMINAL!*

Somebody having authority over me?

NO!

Where I needed to be on my best behavior and answer questions on demand.

Legal consequences on the line?

NO!

I CAN CONTROL MY OWN DESTINY. I'M NOT PUTTING MYSELF IN THIS POSITION EVER AGAIN!

Right at that moment was a *tipping point!*

Eyes Wide Open

"This was the time in my life that I realized who I was and what my future should look like. Dave, Daddy's lifestyle, for me, wasn't intriguing as much. All the 'bloom came off the rose,' and my mind immediately went in a different direction. At that moment, I had Mommy's voice ringing in my ears."

This was the second answer to my earlier question, "How do you come back from that?"

Well, I believe, I clearly did.

Parting Shot

It's been said that the formative years of a person's life and what they are taught can set the foundation for one's personality traits and beliefs for a lifetime.

I know it's also true that life experiences can alter that to some degree.

However, I feel if you were raised with moral convictions and adhere to your beliefs, then the many curve balls that life throws will allow you to maintain consistency in your thinking.

For example, the kid in the inner city chooses not to be part of any gang or fall to a life of crime.

It's easier and more popular to follow. So why don't they?

Because he/she has a strong inner belief of who they are. That came from people who spoke to their heart and soul when they were young.

I believe that never leaves you, and it was the same for me! I realized who I was at that exact moment with Agent Finnegan.

In my personal journey, I always leaned on my earlier teachings and lessons that were taught to me by my mom.

I hope and pray I have that same effect on my children. I like to think I do.

Simply put, I would not be who I am today without recognizing and responding to experiences in my life that I refer to as my Tipping Point.

10

One Last Laugh

Cousin finally emerged from the bathroom. It seemed like he was in there for a lifetime. He walked over to me and Dave with this Cheshire grin.

As he sat down next to me, I said, "Cousin, I thought you fell in. And what the fuck you so happy about?"

He had a look like the weight of the world came off his shoulders. He proudly proclaimed, "Michael, wow I feel like a million dollars! I just took some dump. I was on the throne and..."

I quickly interrupted and shouted, "Ok, got it, don't give me the details!"

I don't know what it is with us men. We view defecating like we just encountered a religious experience. Men also love to articulate the process and give you the blow-by-blow. No matter what the age, we rate and rank each episode like it's the Olympics™.

I guess it's a passage to manhood.

Santa Claus

As Cousin was trying to tell us about his bathroom conquest, John came over and handed him the check.

Cousin looked puzzled, "What the fuck is this?"

Dave looked at him laughing and said, "Big shot, you won The Yankee bet and you said beers on me."

Cousin again was confused and replied, "What am I, Santa Claus?"

I laughed. "Today you are. Just pay the check, you cheap fuck."

On command, Cousin reached into his pocket and pulled out his credit card.

I felt kind of bad, so I said, "Cousin, if it makes you feel better, I got the tip."

With that being said, I left John with a handsome tip, and we reluctantly headed out for our final destination.

On the Road Again

We slowly made our way to the now full parking lot and continued our journey to the penitentiary. There was now a light drizzle, and the time was 12:33 p.m. We had a half-hour till Lewisburg, just like we planned it.

I jumped in the driver's seat, and we resumed our road trip.

While driving, I noticed that we needed gas and air in one of the tires. There was a station just a few blocks from Hanks, so I pulled in.

I was confused and said to Dave and Cousin, "How the hell are we low on air?"

Cousin yelled back, "Wouldn't it be a kick in the ass if somebody in the parking lot let some of it out?"

I thought, *Hmm who knows? We have New York plates.*

We pulled into the station, got a full tank of gas, and then I drove over to the air pump. By looking at the air gauge on the dashboard, we didn't need much, so I jumped out, filled the tire, and within three minutes, we were ready to go.

Putting air in the tire sparked my memory, and I said, "This brings back a story."

We were all nervous about what we were about to experience at Lewisburg. I felt we needed to laugh off this nervous energy and try not to dwell on our current circumstance.

"Cuz, Dave knows this story, so I'm directing this to you."

With a hint of sarcasm, Cuz said, "Ok, here we go again."

A Long Island Tale

"Cousin, we were living with my grandparents in Lindenhurst, Long Island. It was right before Grace was born, so I must have been four months shy of my sixth birthday. Dave, you were in school, so I was bored all day. Remember, I hadn't started school due to the age cutoff in Long Island. I had a lot of time to kill, and on top of that, I was a hyper little fuck, so being bored, I would roam the streets looking to cause havoc. It was a different world back then. Young kids weren't supervised like they are today; the world was a safer place."

Cousin whispered, "Sad but true."

"Cousin, my mom would tell me, 'Stay in front of the house.' She thought I was playing out front, but unbeknownst to her, I was canvassing my block, looking for cars to take air out of the tires."

Cousin was yelling, "What?! Really?! Damn, you were a little gangster!"

"Every day, I would hit two or three cars and do it again the following day. After about a week, I got about every car, except for one. Reason being, every time I would reach down to get the back tire (I liked getting the back ones), the homeowner's dog would bark like crazy. I could never complete the job out of fear the owner would hear the dog and come out and catch me. Truth be told, I was getting frustrated!"

Cousin chimed in, "Frustrated? You were five!"

Laughing, I said, "I know it's crazy, but I was on a mission. This went on for days. I got each one, but this fucking car was the last one standing! Day after day, I would try, but nothing! Until finally, I had enough!"

"I will never forget. I was out on my block, and I had to fucking pee so bad. I didn't want to go back home because I wanted to GET THIS DONE!"

Warning! Warning! Elvis Reference

"So, I walked up to the car, and I started taking the air out. The dog is barking like crazy, but I didn't care. Remember, I got to pee!"

"So, with my left hand, I'm holding on to my 'Little Elvis' (that's what little boys do. Well, sometimes the older ones too), fighting off the urge to go."

"With my right, I'm bending low and taking the air out. The dog was going crazy, but like I said, I was on a mission, and nothing was going to stop me! Come to think of it, it may have been a hound dog…"

The Hand of Justice?

"Cuz, suddenly, the homeowner came up from behind me and yelled, 'Hey! You little bastard!'"

"Before I could run away, he grabbed the back of my shirt, stopped me, and slapped me on my ass. HARD!"

"Well, after he hit me, I just let go and peed my pants."

Cousin was now freaking, "That guy hit you! You peed! What?!"

"Yep, I got away and ran home, and when I got to my grandparents' house, I just went inside and changed quick. I didn't want my mother to find out what happened. She would have hit me harder than that asshole. I changed and thought, *Ok, it's over, what's done is done.*"

"Wouldn't you know, this moron called the cops on me, and around a half-hour later, the cops came to my grandparents' house! I remember sitting on the steps inside the house by the front door. Through the stained glass, I could see the police siren lights flickering."

Cousin asked, "Wait, Michael, the cops had the siren lights on for a five-year-old kid taking air out of car tires?"

Laughing, I said, "Yes! Unbelievable but true."

"All I can hear is my grandfather, Dominic, yelling and the cops trying to hold him back. He wanted to kick the shit out of the neighbor who hit me! He could have cared less about what I did. He just wanted to give this prick some payback. My grandfather was right, who the hell was this guy to put his hand on me? Without a doubt, I would react the same way if somebody ever put a hand on my grandson! So, Cousin, that's my story, and I'm sticking to it."

Cousin asked, "Come on, did this really happen?"

"Every single word! Eventually, the cops left, and I thought I was going to catch hell from my mother and grandfather. But to my surprise, I didn't. When they came in, they both didn't say a word, and we had dinner. They probably thought the guy was an asshole and got what he deserved."

A Little Sarcasm

"Now, Cousin, are you happy I told you this story? Mister, here we go again?"

Cousin said, "Yes, that was a good one." Then he jokingly whispered, "This fucking guy..."

We all just laughed.

One of Many Side Bars

I feel humor is good medicine to offset life's difficult moments. We all face many; therefore, I think the trick is to find the best way to navigate them. Not that it's a cure-all, but putting a smile on others' faces and sharing a laugh might create much-needed temporary amnesia. Like I mentioned earlier, I was dealing with many conflicting emotions on this trip, and Dave, Cousin, and I were looking for and needed a little escape.

I looked at the GPS on my dash, and it said we had about twenty minutes till the penitentiary. I just wanted to keep on laughing, putting off the inevitable sadness and grief. We began to reminisce and talk about people from our past. We just wanted to share an idle conversation. I think we were all just afraid of silence, so we just kept on yapping.

Cousin

Cousin was a great addition to have on this particular road trip. He was kind of the comic relief that Dave and I needed. Not that he's a clown—far from it—but he was smart enough to realize what was required, and he played the role.

I appreciate his insight, much love and forever grateful to him.

Hey, that's what families do. No?

John L. Sullivan

Cousin, still laughing from the tire story, said, "Michael, keep 'em coming, we need another."

"Ok, Cuz, as you know, hanging around my father, I would meet many characters. Some of them were interesting and intriguing; others were right out of Hollywood casting. Let me tell you about a guy that could have been straight out of a *Looney Tunes* cartoon.

"My father had a friend, and he lived on the Lower East Side of Manhattan. He was an older Jewish street guy and was told in his day, not to be messed with. Someone we called an Old Timer. Never forget his name—Lershsky."

Cousin said, "Lershky? What the?"

I laughed, "I know, that was his name. Not sure if it was a nickname. Anyway, it's not important."

"Cuz, whenever he was in someone's company and was introduced, his greeting was quite unlike any other. For example, my father said, 'Michael, I would like you to meet Lershky.' I would extend my hand for a handshake."

"He would extend his, and right when we shook hands, he would say, 'Shake the hand that shook the hand of John L. Sullivan. The first heavyweight champ of the world.' I guess I was surprised—I wasn't expecting that response. I kind of laughed, and my father shook his head to extend my hand again."

"So, on cue, I did. I put my hand out again, and we shook."

"SHAKE THE HAND THAT SHOOK THE HAND OF JOHN L. SULLIVAN. THE FIRST HEAVYWEIGHT CHAMP OF THE WORLD!"

"I was like, 'What the fuck?' Apparently, this was this guy's routine with everyone, whether it was hellos or goodbyes."

Cousin asked, "John L. Sullivan? Was he really the first heavyweight champ? I never heard of him."

"Cuz, I also never heard of this guy, so I went home and looked him up in an encyclopedia. He was a real guy, and he was the first champ from 1882-1892. Fucking guy died in 1918!"

Dave was laughing, "Wow, that's a real old timer. That was a time and place with people that can never be duplicated."

I couldn't have agreed more...

Lesson 101

Another lesson for you post-boomers: An encyclopedia was a series of books that provided information on history or any topic needed. Kind of like what Google provides today, except you couldn't get the information in a split second from the palm of your hand.

Ahh, technology—are we really better off today?

Sometimes, I miss the good old days and its people.

What do you think?

Mama Justice...Italian Style

"Cuz, here's another quick one. This one is about Grandma Josie."

Dave said, "If it's the one that I think it is, Cousin, hold onto your hat!"

Just a little background on Grandma Josie. She was my father's mom and married to Diamond. A high-strung, no-nonsense woman, tough as they come. She did not take shit from anyone!

Remember earlier when I mentioned she cut Diamond's lip with a paring knife? Well, that was just a small sample of Grandma Josie.

"Cuz, my father told me this one, so it was way before my time."

"Every night when my father and uncle were little kids, my grandmother would bathe them, dress them in pajamas, and put them to bed. Just a normal routine performed nightly. Well, as the story goes, one night my grandmother noticed that my uncle had black and blue marks all over his leg. She questioned my uncle and father, and neither said anything."

Omertà—a Sicilian code of silence.

"My grandmother pressed the question again because she thought she saw hand marks as bruises. After the third time she asked forcefully, my uncle finally cracked and told her that a nun at their Catholic school had hit him."

"Cuz, you remember back in the day in Catholic schools. If students misbehaved, they would be slapped and hit with rulers as a form of discipline."

Dave interrupted, "How the heck was that acceptable? I remember in first grade in Lindenhurst, a nun hit me with a ruler on my hand. It hurt for days, but the nuns were given the fucking green light. Looking back, it was strange that parents didn't have a problem with it. For some crazy reason, it was a form of teaching and discipline."

I continued the story. "When my grandmother found out a nun hit my uncle and left those bruises, all hell broke loose." (No pun intended.) She asked my uncle the name of the nun, and he told her it was Sister Giovanna. All the kids and faculty called her Sister Gia."

"The next day, my grandmother went to the school, walked in calmly, and sought out Sister Gia, whom she found participating in a fire drill with the students. She was chaperoning her class in the hallway in the direction of the stairs. Well, Cuz, my grandmother announced who she was, and then she proceeded to grab the nun by her collar, drag her, and then she threw her down a flight of stairs!"

Cousin went nuts. "WHAT?! She did what?!"

"Yep, she threw her down a flight of stairs! I explained. "She also told Sister Gia that if she ever touched her son again, she would come back and throw her down another flight of stairs! Wouldn't you know, my uncle and father were never touched again!"

Dave laughed, "I told you to hold onto your hat!"

Cousin was now going ballistic. "Your grandmother was the O.G.! Talk about street justice. Michael, that's Mama justice!"

We all really enjoyed this story.

It was hard to believe, but unfortunately for Sister Gia, it was true. I guess she had it coming.

Sometimes, God works in mysterious ways.

Don't you think?

A Quick Reflection

Looking at the GPS on the dash, I noticed we still had about ten minutes to go. We had time for one more story before this image I had of my father would become reality.

I was at the point of this trip thinking, *What is the experience of seeing the lifeless body of my father going to be like?*

It's the anxious moments prior to the unknown. I didn't want my mind to get tangled with these emotions, so I had one last story before Lewisburg.

"Guys, one more Diamond story?"

Dave and Cuz simultaneously said, "Let's have it!"

Another Diamond Classic

"Ok, we have ten minutes. I'll make this quick. I was working at Grace 2, and it was around four o'clock in the afternoon when this gigantic guy came walking into the store. Guy could have played in the NBA. He had to be around six-foot-six, maybe seven."

Big!

"Anyway, he ordered a slice and a soda, but I could only see him from the waist up because the pizza counter was blocking his lower half. I will never forget. It was summer, so he was only wearing a T-shirt, and he was wearing some type of fatigue pants. The guy must have thought he was in the Amazon or something! If I could have seen his full attire, I never would have served him."

"Anyway, I was working with Johnny 'The Pie Man.'"

Cuz interrupted and said, "Sure, the little Italian guy—right off the boat—built like a bull."

Quick Tutorial

Johnny was an Italian immigrant who had just come to America maybe five years prior and spoke with a heavy accent. Italian Americans like Dave, Cuz, and myself call these people, Right Off the Boat.

Back to the Story

"Yeah Cuz, that Johnny. Anyway, I hand this Amazon guy his pizza and soda and say, 'Seventy-five cents.'"

Cuz yelled out, "Seventy-five cents?! What is this, 1956?!"

I laughed and said, "No, idiot, 1976. Let me continue, we only have about seven minutes."

"The guy takes the pizza and soda and says word for word, 'Fuck you, I got no money.' I was stunned, so I asked him again, and he told me the same thing."

"I was only fourteen, but I was smart enough to know that this Amazon guy would crush me like a grape. So, I turned to Johnny and quickly relayed the story to him. I thought, Well, maybe the two of us could take him."

Johnny approached him and in his broken accent said, "What? You don't wanna pay?"

"The guy told him to fuck off, so we both came around the counter to confront him. It was inside the store, and we had customers. Now I could see how he was dressed. He had fatigues that he had cut to three-fourths length, and he was barefoot."

"So, we told him to go outside, and we followed him out. We were ready to fight this behemoth, and we squared off in the middle of the street. Across from Grace 2, there were luxury apartments with big balconies. As we were facing off, I noticed there were many people sitting on their balconies about to enjoy the show."

"Guys, right before we were going in for the attack, the guy picked up a bottle to use as a weapon."

Johnny yelled to me, "Go get the pizza peel on the top of the oven!"

Teaching moment: The pizza peel is the wooden shovel used to take the cooked pizza out of the oven.

Back to Diamond

"I ran into the store, and in my excitement of getting back out there, I dropped the peel right by the door, and it broke into pieces. It was like a comedy skit."

"I picked up the pieces, handed two to Johnny, and I took the others. We faced off with this guy in the middle of the street with an audience looking on from the balconies. He lunged at us with the bottle, and in my nervous excitement, I panicked and threw my broken pizza peel at him. Johnny saw this and did the same, but now we had no weapons."

"So, we did the smart thing and retreated! We both ran back into the store. There was a construction site across the street, and this 'Amazon man' walked over and picked up a brick. Now we're thinking he's going to throw the brick through the store's window. Johnny locked the door, and I did the smart thing...I called Diamond."

"He was working at Grace 1, which was only about seven blocks away. It was literally a two-minute drive because with Diamond driving, the lights didn't matter, he was breaking every one!"

"It was previously planned that Diamond was picking me up at five to take me home. Grace 1 closed every night at six, and whenever I worked at Grace 2, he was my ride home. I called Diamond and quickly told him about our situation."

He yelled, "Mikey, no problem, I'll be right there! I swear, within a minute, his white Cadillac came screaming up the block. In the car, he had four baseball bats (family tradition) and Tony 'The Pie Man.' He was another guy Right Off the Boat that was no taller than five feet four."

(A pie man is a guy who makes pizza pies.)

"Diamond jumps out of the Caddy, hands each guy a bat, and yelled, 'Mikey, where is this cocksucker?!'"

Cousin yelled out, "This is fucking nuts!"

The Chase

"Guys, let me set this up. There were four of us, with Diamond being sixty-six years old. We had two Right Off the Boat pie men, both no taller than five-foot-four, and then there was me, a fourteen-year-old kid."

"This is what we had to go to war with against this monster!"

"I yelled to Diamond, 'There he is!'"

"Diamond yells out to the guy, 'You motherfucker, I'm going to break every bone in your body!'"

"What happened next surprised the hell out of me. The guy sees Diamond, looks like he just saw a ghost, and takes off running! No shoes, and the guy was running like he was in the Olympics™! Guy could have been a hurdler!"

"Remember, Diamond at the time was sixty-six!"

I guess it's all in the delivery?!

"So, with bats in hand, we start chasing this guy down the street. The people on the balconies were going crazy, cheering. The two pie men were out front, and Diamond and I were running behind. I wanted to run with Diamond because of his age, and, well, he was my protector."

Stupid I wasn't.

"In the background, with all this going on, the Twin Towers—World Trade Center—looked down upon us."

Whenever I worked at Grace 2, those buildings were always in my line of sight. For some reason, I always had such an emotional connection to The Twin Towers.

RETREAT!

"Out of nowhere, Diamond says to me, 'Mikey, slow up, I gotta be careful with my heart.' Upon command, I slowed down, and we walked back to the pizzeria."

"Within five minutes of returning to the store, Diamond and I see the two Right Off the Boat five-foot-four pie men running back towards us, bats still in hand, looking like they were running for their lives!"

"Cousin, when the pie men got back, they told us this bare-footed monster saw a small tree that had two large wooden poles holding it in place. The guy, being so strong, was able to pull one of those big poles right out of the ground to use as a weapon!"

Dave was hysterical, and Cuz yelled out, "What the—?!"

I yell back, "Cuz, what the is right! For some crazy reason, the guy stopped chasing the pie men, and he didn't come back to the pizzeria."

Oh...It Gets Better

"It's now just about five o'clock, which means it's time for Diamond to take me home. I'm thinking, Okay, I dodged a bullet, it's over, time to go. I jump into Diamond's Caddy, and we start to head out. Out of the corner of my eye, I see the guy walking, and I'm hoping Diamond doesn't see him."

"Guys, at this point, I just wanted to go home!"

Back to good old Corona.

"But *nooooooo*, Diamond sees him and yells, 'Mikey, there's the cocksucker!' He floors the car, and now he's trying to run this guy down. It's crazy. You can't make this shit up, and within a second, the Amazon man takes off like a deer."

Cuz yelled out, "Deer Hunter!"

I laughed back, "No, not quite, but close."

"He's now running for his life and heads into one of the luxury apartment buildings with a twenty-four-hour doorman. Diamond literally drives up on the sidewalk, jumps out, and goes after this guy inside the building. So, I see this and do exactly the same. I'm like, 'Jeez, here we go again. I thought this was over.'"

"This monster of a guy is now cowering behind the doorman. He's frightened of this sixty-six-year-old man!"

I'm telling you—it's all about the delivery.

"The doorman is threatening to call the cops, having no idea we know *all* the cops. They were used to dealing with Diamond." (Remember Kunta Kinte?)

"I step in front of Diamond and try to defuse the situation by holding him back. I said, 'Diamond, let it go, c'mon.'"

"He breaks away and yells, 'C'mon?! Mikey, I'll kick you in the fucking belly!'"

"Cousin, at that point, I remember saying to myself, Go ahead, go kill yourself, I was done!"

Dave and Cousin are smiling from ear to ear.

"After maybe about a minute, Diamond calmed down, and we got back in the car and headed home. Within a minute, he was laughing and kidding with me like nothing happened."

Just like when I was a kid in his house in Jackson Heights...

ABSOLUTELY CRAZY!

You gotta love him!

It's a Long Way Home

Diamond driving me home now meant I had to say my prayers. Remember I told you earlier about Diamond's cough? Well, he would cough sometimes while driving. This uncontrollable, crazy cough would cause the car to swerve all over the road.

It was like me driving after I hit that deer in Pennsylvania.

It was especially scary when we drove over the Williamsburg Bridge. I envisioned the car driving off the bridge and a day later being scooped up somewhere in Brooklyn.

All I could do was say my Our Fathers and Hail Marys, and with divine intervention, he got me safely home.

Can't make this shit up.

The Wrap-Up

As I finished another Diamond story, we pulled into the penitentiary, its location in the middle of nowhere. As a matter of fact, all the other penitentiaries we visited in the past were located in similar isolated areas.

My heart sank as we drove up to the sign at the entrance that simply read, UNITED STATES PENITENTIARY, LEWISBURG.

After all the shared stories, laughter, and reflective moments, we had finally arrived. All our joy was now gone, knowing what was to come in just a short time. I put my game face on and headed toward the building.

At that moment, I knew I had my One Last Laugh.

11

9/11

The light drizzle of rain had turned into a relentless downpour as we drove through the gates.

The first thing we noticed was the one-hundred-foot guard tower.

Massive. Menacing. A reminder that this place was designed to keep people in, not welcome them.

Lewisburg Penitentiary is an intimidating old brick fortress built in the early 1930s. It looks exactly like the kind of prison you see in movies, the kind of place you never want to call home. We parked the car and made our way to the entrance, a path we had unfortunately walked too many times over the years.

And yet, for some reason...It never felt familiar.

Why?

Because I never wanted to be here.

It's a place where people are locked away, and I was one of the lucky ones who always got to leave. Every time I walked through those doors, I was reminded of the choices I had made. The ones that kept me on the outside.

The right ones.

Herd of Cattle

We reached the visitors entrance, where a long line of people stood waiting to see their loved ones.

The usual crowd. Parents. Wives. Girlfriends. Friends.

But the hardest to see? The children.

Watching them wait for their fathers, clueless about where they really were, always got to me. Their innocence was heartbreaking.

And yet, despite our differences, we were all in the same boat.

No exceptions. No special treatment.

We all followed the same rules, wore the right clothes, and—most importantly—never forgot to bring a bag of quarters. Vending machine currency. The unofficial lifeline of every visit.

It wasn't just snacks in those machines. They stocked everything: microwave meals, sandwiches, drinks. The early birds grabbed the good stuff. If you were late, you were stuck with the scraps. You learn the system fast. First-timers usually didn't know the drill, but there was always someone around to help. If you needed change, you could count on a stranger to swap your bills for quarters.

There was an unspoken camaraderie here. A strange, silent understanding.

A brotherhood.

A secret society of the forgotten.

Lewisburg Penitentiary

We walked through the doors marked VISITORS ONLY and approached the front desk. Two prison guards sat behind it, their job simple to check IDs, confirm visitor lists, and make sure no one smuggled in anything prohibited.

Weapons. Drugs. Food.

In the past, we had gotten away with sneaking in snacks. But today, there was no need.

We knew the drill. Pat-downs. Metal detectors. Standard procedure.

The guard checking us in was a big guy named Officer Bruckner. His uniform was tight across his chest, and he looked like he could start for the New York Giants.

A "Hack." That's the inmate lingo for a prison guard.

My father had always been polite to the Hacks but never too friendly. Just kept his head down. Did his time.

Prison Protocol

Dave, Cuz, and I handed over our driver's licenses and emptied our pockets, preparing for the metal detector. Same routine as the airport.

Officer Bruckner studied our IDs, then hesitated. He glanced up. "Only one of you is allowed inside today."

We exchanged looks.

"Only the next of kin can enter," he explained, his tone professional but firm.

And that next of kin? Me.

Dave and Cuz weren't on the list.

Cuz shrugged. He wasn't thrilled about it, but let's be honest, identifying a dead body wasn't on anyone's bucket list.

But Dave? That was different.

I turned to him. "Dave, I'm sorry. I had no idea it would just be me. I thought Daddy would have listed all three of us."

Officer Bruckner cleared his throat. "Federal protocol. Only one person can do the official identification. Looks like your dad picked you."

I felt awful. Dave deserved his goodbye just as much as I did.

But he just shook his head and whispered, "Let's just get him home. I'm fine."

I appreciated that. He was stepping up, being the big brother, making it easier for me. We hugged, and I handed him my car keys.

Bruckner said, "It should take about an hour. You'll sign the paperwork, confirm the release, and indicate the funeral home."

I nodded. "I'll call you as soon as I'm done."

Cuz gave me a sheepish grin. Then they turned and walked back to the car.

Once through the metal detector, Bruckner returned my ID, phone, and cash. No need for quarters.

Unfortunately, this visit didn't require vending machine snacks. Usually, phones weren't allowed inside, but given the circumstances, he let me keep it.

Brotherly Love

Bruckner led me down a long corridor toward an office where I'd meet with a prison official and sign the release paperwork.

As we walked, I texted Grace.

I'm here. I'll call you soon.

She wanted to be here, but she couldn't leave Mom. Leukemia had already weakened her. Early-stage dementia made things worse. Leaving her alone wasn't an option. Watching Mom struggle had been one of the hardest things I'd ever experienced. She had always been my guiding light in a dark room, the one who kept me grounded, the one who reminded me of who I really was.

And now Grace had become her caretaker.

Every single day, I was grateful for my sister.

I felt her absence like a weight in my chest. She was my spiritual ally, my partner in crime in every way that mattered.

We had each other's backs. Always had. Always would.

People like Grace? They don't grow on trees.

I knew that. And I hoped she knew it too.

The Middle Child, A Different Twist

I joked earlier about "Middle Child Syndrome" and all that perfection bullshit.

But the truth? Being the middle child means you get to wear two different hats.

You're both the younger sibling and the older one, and at times the dynamics can be vastly different. And if you're a middle child, you know exactly what I mean. At the end of the day, we're each one-third perfection, making us one hundred percent as a whole.

Amen.

The Waiting Game

At the end of what felt like an endless corridor, Officer Bruckner led me into an empty office.

A metal placard on the door read in bold letters: INMATE ADMINISTRATION. He gestured for me to take a seat and said, "Administrator Victoria Milo will be with you shortly."

I thanked him and sat in a stiff chair in front of a metal and wood veneer desk.

The office was sterile, unwelcoming. The walls were a harsh, government-issue white. The floor was a cheap beige linoleum. The fluorescent lights overhead buzzed like an old bug zapper.

Exactly what you'd expect from a prison office.

I had no idea how long I'd be waiting, so I pulled out my phone to call Toni. Just as I was about to dial, I noticed from my app that she was at her sister's house. Not exactly a place for a private conversation. Instead, I sent her a quick text with an update.

It's crazy how much technology has changed in my lifetime.

The time on my phone read 2:15 p.m.

I decided to call Grace.

A Comforting Voice

Grace picked up on the first ring. "Spud," she said, using her nickname for me. "What's going on? You okay?"

I kept my voice low. "Yeah, as good as can be. Just waiting for the prison administrator so I can sign some papers. It's been a long day."

"I bet."

"I'm solo. I haven't seen Daddy yet. Dave and Cuz weren't on the accepted visitors list."

She sounded confused. "Really? Why?"

"For some reason, Daddy listed only me as the next of kin."

She let out a breath. "Spud, are you sure you're okay doing this alone?"

"Yeah, I'm good. Appreciate your concern." I changed the subject. "How's Mommy?"

Grace sighed. "She's getting weaker. More forgetful. Her anxiety is worse. Her doctor called it 'Sundown Syndrome' and says symptoms get worse at sunset."

We both sat with the weight of it all—our mom's decline, our dad's sudden death. It was a lot.

Then Grace added, "Spud, do you remember my next-door neighbor Jimmy?"

"Of course. The fireman. He was at your house last Christmas. Why?"

Her voice dropped. "He passed away last night."

I felt my stomach sink. "No..."

"Yeah. Fifty-seven years old."

New York's Bravest

Jimmy had been a New York City firefighter. Like so many first responders from 9/11, he developed serious health issues years later.

When called upon, these men and women rushed into danger without hesitation. They served their city and their country.

They should and always will be cherished.

The heroes of that day—those who were at the Trade Center or helped in the cleanup at Ground Zero—are an inspiration. A model of the American and New York spirit.

You can't overuse the word 'hero' when describing them.

I felt helpless, knowing nothing I could say would change the tragedy of Jimmy's passing. But I knew what mattered. "Grace, please pass my condolences to his wife and family."

A beat of silence.

"I feel so sad being surrounded by sickness, heartache, and grief. First with Mommy slowly deteriorating, then Daddy suddenly passing and now Jimmy."

I could feel her heaviness through the phone.

She continued, "You were so close to the Trade Center on 9/11, weren't you?"

"Four blocks away."

"I never really knew that. If I had, I would've lost my mind."

I could hear the emotion in her voice. "We never talked about what that day was like for you."

I exhaled slowly. "You really want to know?"

She did. And truthfully, I needed to talk. My nervous energy was only growing while I waited for the administrator.

We had always been there for each other. And this time would be no different.

An Unforeseen Tragedy

"Okay, Grace, I'll start from the beginning of the day. Toni and I traveled into the city together from Long Island, and our train was delayed twenty minutes. No big deal, just another commuter annoyance."

"When we arrived at Penn Station, Toni went uptown, and I headed downtown to Wall Street. We kissed quickly, and she left for work."

"Toni was working at JP Morgan, and just a few months prior, her office had moved from Wall Street to 63rd Street and Fifth Ave. Thank God she wasn't working downtown that day. I hopped on the number two subway to Wall Street. Just a fifteen-minute ride. I remember it so clearly."

"The stop before Wall Street was Chambers Street. When the train pulled into Chambers, it didn't move for about ten minutes. The doors stayed open."

Grace asked, "Did you get nervous just sitting there?"

"A little," I admitted. "It was weird."

"Chambers Street station sits directly beneath or very close to the World Trade Center. Finally, the doors shut, and the train rolled forward."

"I didn't know it yet, but the first plane had hit the towers at that exact moment. When I arrived at Wall Street, everything seemed normal."

(Underground, you're disconnected from the world. You have no clue what's happening above.)

"I climbed the stairs and started my three-block walk to my office at 2 Wall Street. Trinity Church was my first sight, like every day. It was a warm pre-fall morning, not a cloud in the sky. But then I saw something strange."

"Tiny bits of paper floating in the air, almost like confetti. Ticker-tape parade style. What the fuck? I thought."

"Something wasn't right. As I neared my office, the pieces of burnt paper were everywhere.

One of my co-workers stood outside having a cigarette. I asked him what was going on. He told me, like everyone assumed at the time, that a small plane had hit the World Trade Center."

"Horrible. A freak accident. My first thought? The pilot must've had a heart attack mid-flight."

Office Chaos and Confusion

"I took the elevator to the ninth floor. Everyone in my office was talking about the plane crash. From my window, I had a clear view of the towers, with only a cemetery separating us. I saw flames pouring out of one of the buildings. And I remember thinking, That's a big hole for a small plane. What the fuck?"

"I walked to the coffee room, chatting with coworkers, when my office phone rang. It was Mommy. Which never happened."

Grace interrupted, "Wait. Mommy called you that day?"

"She did. She was worried about the news reports and wanted to make sure I was okay." I reassured her. "Mom, I'm fine. Nothing to worry about."

"Then, just as I hung up the phone, BOOM. The entire building shook like an earthquake."

Terrorist Attack, Pure Fucking Evil

"I ran back to my office window. That's when I saw the second plane explode into the other tower. At that moment, we all knew. This was no accident. It was a terrorist attack."

"I grabbed my phone and called Toni. 'I'm leaving the building,' I told her. 'I'll stay in touch. Whatever you do, do not leave your office until I get uptown.' We had no idea what was coming next. I didn't want her traveling alone."

"The office was in full-blown panic mode. Some people wanted to stay. The firm's owner wanted to wait for an official statement about the stock market. To me, that was a head-scratcher.

"OF COURSE THE MARKET WAS CLOSING! WE JUST EXPERIENCED A TERRORIST ATTACK! ARE YOU THAT FUCKING STUPID?!"

"Grace, our building was right across from the New York Stock Exchange, so I told my coworkers we needed to leave and they agreed. I suggested we take the stairs in case of another attack. If the power went out, we didn't want to be stuck in an elevator."

"We headed toward South Street Seaport, hoping to find a restaurant with a TV for news updates. As we walked, I called Toni again. 'I'm okay,' I told her. 'I'm heading uptown.'"

Heroes

"I'll never forget passing a firehouse and seeing firefighters rush toward the Twin Towers."

"I was moving away from danger. They were running into it. I'm sure many of those brave men never made it out. That image will stay with me forever."

I Can't Figure Out Some People—Fucking Idiots

"Then I noticed something that pissed me off. Crowds of people standing and staring at the towers. Watching as workers trapped inside jumped to their deaths. Like it was some kind of spectacle. What the fuck?!"

"Have some fucking respect!" I was livid. "This wasn't a goddamn sporting event."

Grace yelled, "Michael, that's exactly how I would've felt!"

One of the Good Ones

"I was with my coworkers—four women and my friend, Steve, Wade's assistant at the time."

Grace chimed in, "Oh my God, Wade! What a great person."

She's right. Wade is one of the good ones. A second brother to me.

Loyal. Trustworthy.

We've been business partners for twenty-three years and counting. God willing.

Special people don't grow on trees.

And Wade? He's one of them.

When I first met him and heard his name, I remember thinking, *Hmmm... Wade?* Not a lot of those running around Queens...

Horror

"Grace, I'm not sure when this administrator is coming, so let me finish the story."
"We got to South Street Seaport only to find the restaurants closed, with no access to the media to figure out what was really going on."

"Steve and I felt our co-workers had calmed down, so it was time for me to leave and head uptown to meet Toni. From there, we'd get out of the city and back to Long Island. Steve asked if he could come with me. I said sure, and we started the long journey to 63rd Street."

"We had barely walked five blocks from The Seaport when the first tower came down. Chaos erupted in the streets. People ran for their lives. I turned back and saw thick, black smoke swallowing everything behind us."

"The bright, beautiful day turned to darkness in a second. I wanted to go back and check on my co-workers, but it was impossible. I felt sick to my stomach. At that moment, I thought those women were dead. Then, a gigantic plume of smoke came barreling toward us."

Hunkered In

"I grabbed Steve. 'Let's get off the street. This can't be healthy.' We ducked into a nearby building just in time."

"A thin layer of toxic soot covered our suits, but compared to the people outside, we got lucky.

We headed into the basement offices, where we finally had access to a landline. By then, the first tower had collapsed, cutting off cell service."

"I called Toni. No answer. Now I was really worried. I knew I could control my own fate but hers? I had no control over that."

"Grace, does that make any sense?"

She answered quickly. "Yes!"

"Unable to reach Toni, I called Wade. He was already home, having caught the last train out of the city before everything shut down. He told me the news was reporting six unaccounted planes in the sky."

"I remember thinking, what the hell is going to happen next? For the first time in my life, I felt true hopelessness."

"Minutes later, we found out the second tower had collapsed. It was like déjà vu. I was stuck again. Just like in the subway tunnel earlier. No windows, no idea what was happening outside."

Death and Destruction

"I finally reached Toni. Told her I'd call again before heading out. Told her, 'Please, hold tight. I'm coming.'"

"With the second tower now gone, Steve and I agreed to wait for the smoke, soot, and debris to settle. Three hours passed before we stepped outside."

"Someone handed us small, ripped towels to use as makeshift masks. I grabbed extra. Tied two around Steve's face, he did the same for me, and we began our journey uptown. The streets were eerily silent."

"The sky had cleared, but everything was covered in an inch of gray dust. Like a snowfall in September. As we walked, police warned us to stay away from federal buildings and garbage cans."

"Bomb threats were everywhere. No one knew what to believe. Rumors spread like wildfire. With every step, my emotions intensified."

"Rage. Heartbreak. Disbelief. I was angry. These people had attacked our city. Our country. Our people. Steve and I made a silent agreement. We wouldn't look back at where the towers once stood. That space deserved respect."

Sad.

Mom Calling

Grace suddenly interrupted. "Hold on, Mom's calling."

Whenever Mom called, we dropped everything.

I held the line. And then...

A wave of emotions hit me like a ton of bricks.

Sometimes Life Takes Away Your Innocence

The towers crumbling down felt like the end of something more than just buildings.

I thought back to my younger years. The days when life still felt innocent.

Back then, who the hell would've predicted this? Where the fuck is humanity?

Lost. Buried. Forgotten.

I remembered what the towers had meant to me. How their lights comforted me when I delivered pizzas late at night, guiding me through the dark, dangerous streets.

I had watched them being built. From the windows of Grace 2, I had a front-row seat to their rise.

They became *icons.* A symbol of New York. Of America.

But to me? They were just part of the neighborhood. Familiar. Constant.

And now?

Gone. Gutted.

I thought about Toni.

About the old pictures of the towers I bought from a street vendor for her when we were just kids.

I thought about Diamond. About chasing that big guy through the streets, the towers standing
tall in the background.

If buildings could talk, they probably would've said, "Oh shit, here we go again."

I thought about making pizza at Grace 2, the towers always in my line of sight. They were woven into the fabric of my life.

Now, all of it is gone.

The towers. The pizza places.

Diamond.

My father.

It felt like the end of innocence.

Human Beings Are A Confusing Puzzle

Grace came back on the phone, "Michael, sorry. No worries, Mommy's fine. She just wanted to know what time later I was stopping by."

The three minutes I was on hold pulled me right back to that horrible day. I realized a chapter of my life had shut that day.

I was emotionally spent.

I took a deep breath and continued. "Okay, Grace, where was I? Oh yes, as we were heading uptown, I passed the location where Grace 1 was, and my heart sank. Everything that came before felt so distant. Those memories didn't seem to matter much now."

"As we walked, we passed through The Diamond Exchange. I wanted access to a landline phone to call Toni and let her know where I was. We entered a jewelry store. The employees sat in a circle, angry because business was closed due to the attack."

"I explained my situation. Their body language told me I wasn't welcome. They could give a fuck. I wasn't a paying customer."

"I was surprised. Disappointed. I politely explained that I was coming from the World Trade Center area and unable to use my cell phone. I just needed a quick call to my wife. Feeling the tension in the room, I promised to keep it short."

"They quickly denied me. I'll never forget it. They yelled, 'NO PHONE FOR YOU!'"

"Grace, WORD FOR FUCKING WORD! MOTHERFUCK-ERS! These people didn't care. They were more worried about the money they weren't making. I thought to myself, Where is humanity? Is it non-existent?"

My "Peeps"...Ahhh NO!

"As we continued, we entered Little Italy. I thought, Hey, these are my people. I'll get a phone here. They're Italians! Cut from the same cloth as me."

"We walked into an Italian deli, a New York institution for nearly a century. I walked up to the owner and explained my situation."

"He smiled and said, 'Sure, no problem. Phone's in the back.' I knew my people wouldn't let me down! Or so I thought."

"I finally reached Toni, started explaining where we should meet. Then wouldn't you know it? After thirty seconds, the owner walked in and said, 'Hey buddy, make it quick, I got deliveries coming in on my fax machine.'"

"I was pissed. What?! Really?! I hung up, disgusted. Human beings were dying. Lives were destroyed. And this asshole was worried about his meatball fucking parm heroes?!"

The same theme—HUMANITY IS DEAD.

And on top of that? FUCK MY PEOPLE.

When the rubber meets the road, you find out who the real ones are.

Reunion

"After that disaster, we continued uptown. I finally met up with Toni. We hugged for a full minute. The relief of being together was indescribable. It had been a long, horrible day. We waited until 6:00 p.m. and caught the train back to Long Island."

Grace was silent for a few seconds. Then she simply said, "Oh my God. Jeez, I never knew."

We spoke for a couple more minutes before she had to prepare lunch and take it to my mother's house. I told her I'd stay in touch and let her know when I was heading back home.

We Will Always Bleed

As I sat quietly in that office, waiting for the administrator, I felt a deep sadness settle in. I thought about how unpredictable life is. How we're constantly blindsided by events we never see coming.

If we were born with the foresight to know our future, we could avoid pain and suffering. But that's not how life works.

Our personal stories are prewritten, unbeknownst to us.

Some say suffering prepares us for future hardships.

I don't buy that bullshit.

We are human. We will always bleed.

There is no magic pill to numb grief. No antidote for loss.

That day taught me a harsh truth. There are many cruel, evil, and selfish people in the world.

But there are also far more good people. And that is what I choose to carry with me.

That gives me peace.

I loved my father and Diamond.

I will never forget them.

Just like I will never forget the innocent souls we lost on 9/11.

12

#07659-143

A Simple Equation

Have you ever wondered how numbers are calculated?

Trust me, I don't spend my days mulling over that. But if you really stop and think about it, numerical equations are methodically derived—whether by applying algebraic formulas to find optimal solutions or by simply accepting that 1+1=2.

These values are computed in a cold, mechanical fashion, whether by calculators, computers, or even memorization. If your memory serves or your calculator's inputs are correct, your answer is spot on. There's no gray area here; the outcome is precise.

No amount of thoughtfulness, critical thinking, or emotional gymnastics is needed to reach a numerical conclusion.

They say numbers don't lie, and that's true. They're nothing but cold, hard facts. In the numbers world, the term 'humane' simply doesn't compute.

Surely, you've heard someone say, "I feel like a number" or "What's the use? I'm just a number."

What they're really saying is that they feel invisible, disconnected, like their voice has been silenced.

A person's name carries humanity, a unique identity that sets them apart. When someone is reduced to a mere number, it's as if society is telling them their humanity has been erased.

That number isn't just a figure; it's a cold, calculated output, a math equation stripped of any human element. I'd love to say that no one should ever reduce a person to a number, but sadly, it happens. And it's a harsh reality no one should have to endure.

Just a Number?

After nearly forty minutes of waiting, Administrator Milo finally burst into her office.

I rose to introduce myself, and she immediately apologized profusely for her delay, citing complications with her previous appointment.

Her courteous, almost congenial demeanor was a refreshing change from my past encounters with prison officials. It was clear she understood the situation, and her empathy was a welcome comfort.

She carried a large, overstuffed folder presumably filled with various forms to sign. When she set it down, the folder hit the desk with a loud thud that echoed through the room.

Sitting across from her, I couldn't help but notice that the beige folder's front cover bore nothing more than a handwritten title: **#07659-143**.

That was it. No name, no additional information. Just a number. I was stunned. Was this man reduced to nothing more than a number?

Bureaucratic Robot

That's when it hit me: Inside that folder lay the details of a human being now reduced to a sterile number.

In an instant, the warm feelings I'd felt toward Administrator Milo evaporated. I wasn't angry with her personally. I simply realized she was just another bureaucratic robot.

My reaction reminded me of my interview with Agent Finnegan. Initially, I felt small, almost inferior beneath the weight of authority. But then, in a flash, I remembered who I was.

Over the years, I've built a rock-solid confidence, self-esteem, and an uncompromising standard for myself.

I felt ten feet tall, looking down on this administrative paper pusher.

I knew that the man detailed in those forms was so much more than a number.

No arbitrary calculation is going to take away his identity and his humanity.

No matter the circumstances or the prejudiced assumptions of so-called "government bobbleheads," I knew deep down that, as a family, our integrity remained untouchable.

I thought to myself, *I may have taken a different path, but I'm ALWAYS FOR THE HOME TEAM!*

I know my people, their stories, and no misguided "higher authority" or bureaucratic protocol can shatter my convictions.

Yet, as I sat there, I realized my anger wasn't aimed at any one individual; it was the system itself that had disillusioned me.

I didn't want this moment to spiral into bitterness; I was searching for peace, solace, and some form of closure in this unorthodox setting. So I took a deep breath, reminded myself that I was simply there to perform my duties and follow the penitentiary's protocol.

I tucked my ego and bravado away and set out to carry out my "Next of Kin Contact" duty.

The Hammer of Justice

You might ask, Why do people put themselves in situations that lead to isolation or even a loss of self?

Why choose a path laden with the risk of demoralizing mental collapse?

Perhaps some react without considering the looming negative outcomes, while others see the consequences but find their moral compass battered and broken by years of disillusionment.

Let's face it. None of us, especially not in the fleeting time we have on this earth, dream of being caged and institutionalized.

Ask any third-grader what they want to be when they grow up, and you won't hear one say, "I want to be in jail."

So, where does it all go wrong?

You might be tempted to say, "They're all just bad people. So what?"

And in many cases, that's not far off.

There are those who murder, rape, and exploit the innocent; villains who, twisted by a warped sense of faith, plan attacks on defenseless lives—9/11 being a grim reminder.

In those instances, I'm right there with anyone who cries out for justice, shouting, "THROW AWAY THE KEY!" without a moment's hesitation.

But not everyone behind bars fits that mold.

Many fall into crime seeking a shortcut, only to later face crushing consequences.

Some stray from the righteous path due to greed and the lure of power; others spiral into addiction and depression, losing their sense of self and spiritual worth in a desperate struggle to survive, ultimately leading to incarceration.

Often, it's just a series of foolish mistakes, blamed on the ignorance of youth.

Please don't misconstrue my words.

I believe in a justice system where those who deserve it receive the hammer of justice.

Yet, like everything else in life, there are shades and levels—each situation must be judged on its own merits.

Evil, however, should never be granted tolerance or forgiveness. That's a judgment for a higher power.

Unwritten Code

If you've been paying attention throughout this story, you know I've never disclosed why my father spent years shuttling in and out of federal prisons.

Even though I chose a different path, I still stick to the unspoken rule that some things are better left unsaid. It's an unwritten code.

Sure, our natural curiosity might be itching for details, but think about it. When you meet someone with a past in jail, do you immediately blurt out, "Hey, why did you go to jail? What did you do?"

NO!

Exactly.

So, in honor of that unspoken code, there's nothing more for me to add.

The Sword of Loyalty

However, I will tell you this.

In life, some people romanticize a certain lifestyle, clinging to a code of ethics, maybe even a blood oath and loyalty that they swear by.

Over time, though, many discover that the path they once idealized isn't nearly as glamorous or lucrative as it first seemed.

So when trouble comes knocking, suddenly rationalization becomes a way to cope with the unanticipated realities.

Hey I'm not one to judge.

I had my share of foresight and hard-earned life lessons that steered me toward what I wanted for my future.

Maybe not everyone was so lucky. Maybe some never acquired the wisdom or experience to learn otherwise. I can't say for sure, and it's above my paygrade to figure it out.

But here's what I know: My father died on the sword of loyalty, and if you ask me, that's not a bad way to go out.

There's your answer to the question why?

If you didn't catch it the first time, go back and read it slowly. It's all there.

A Mike Tyson Punch

I tried to distance myself from that cold, impersonal way of reducing a life to a number.

Yet here I was, watching Administrator Milo methodically open an intimidating folder stuffed with forms. With the precision of someone who's been around the block more than once, she laid everything out on the desk.

As she walked me through each form, the brutal reality struck hard: My father was gone.

In that moment, life morphed into something unrecognizable. I was about to face his lifeless body, and nothing would ever be the same.

We've all had those moments when reality hits you square in the face.

I thought our road trip, filled with reminiscing, laughter, and shared memories, would serve as the emotional exorcism I needed.

Instead, I was hit by a tsunami of grief.

Mike Tyson once said, "Everyone has a plan 'till they get punched in the mouth."

Well, consider that punch delivered.

When life ends so abruptly, there's no time for goodbyes, no chance to process your emotions as you might when watching a loved one battle a terminal illness.

It's like a shot through the heart, leaving you scrambling not to bleed out emotionally.

Protocol and Forms

I never expected the federal government to demand so much paperwork for the Next of Kin process. Officer Bruckner had assured me it would be straightforward.

Instead, I found myself caught in a labyrinth of forms—complex, time-consuming, and utterly draining.

I followed Administrator Milo's lead, signing one form after another.

Oddly enough, as I meticulously dotted every "i" and crossed every "t" on Uncle Sam's documents, I felt a surge of confidence. My father chose me for this duty, and I was determined to honor that trust. No matter how heavy the emotional blow, I wasn't going down without a fight.

After about half an hour of this grim task, I was told to wait for the next, final step in this morbid chain of events.

With her part done, Administrator Milo offered a brief condolence before directing me to wait for Supervisor Doreste, who would escort me to the penitentiary morgue. With the forms signed, the law now demanded that the deceased inmate be properly identified.

A Quick Text

As I sat and waited—because, at that point, that was all I seemed to be doing—I sent off a few texts.

I let Toni know...

Finally done with the paperwork, just waiting to identify my father. Not easy... I never imagined this ending. I'll update you when I'm heading home. I think I'll need a hug. Love and talk later.

I messaged Grace next.

Grace, I'm almost done. Waiting to view Daddy's body. Still can't believe this happened...I signed the paperwork and arranged for the body to be transferred to Carneys Funeral Home in Corona, as we agreed. Love and speak soon.

And I even texted Dave.

Just about finishing up. Give or take 45 minutes.

Asking for Strength

Soon, it was just me and my turbulent thoughts as I awaited the final walk, to face the end of my father's life.

I made the sign of the cross, knelt, and whispered a Hail Mary, pleading for the strength and guidance I desperately needed.

Kneeling there, I searched for solace in my faith, praying to Mother Mary for a spark of divine intervention. I was desperate for refuge; after all, I was in a Federal Penitentiary, a place where even the air seems devoid of comfort or compassion.

Prisons run on cold, calculated routines; they're no sanctuary for a grieving soul. I needed to carve out a small haven within myself, a place of inner peace.

And in that moment of prayer, something shifted. A calm descended upon me, fortifying my spirit and emboldening me to face what lay ahead.

With that newfound inner peace settling in, memories of my father began to flood back. It was as if a higher power was gently prodding me to sift through the fragments of our shared past. Thoughts and recollections ricocheted through my mind, a montage of moments that painted a fuller picture of who my father really was.

A Flashback

I mentioned before that he wasn't always around when I was a kid.

During the time we lived with my grandparents, he ran a bar/lounge near LaGuardia Airport. Working nights meant he was often absent, sparking tensions with my mom.

Driven by impulse, he left the plumber's union to try his hand at business—a risky leap fueled by his unyielding willingness to take chances and his complete lack of fear of failure. In these memories, I found not just the man he was, but the legacy of loyalty and the willingness to throw caution to the wind, that defined him.

It's a trait that's inspired me all my life, and it's the foundation I still stand on today.

It all starts with one simple truth: It takes a leap of faith. If you don't believe in yourself, trust me, nobody else will. I've always admired his never-say-die attitude.

It wasn't just inspiring. It was a call to keep pushing forward. He used to say, "There's a reason God put erasers on pencils."

In other words, sometimes plans don't work out, and you must wipe the slate clean and try again until you get it right.

Believe me, I've wandered through more than a few metaphorical islands before finally landing on my own Plymouth Rock.

You get what I mean, right?

Running a bar/lounge business meant long nights. Late evenings stretched well past three in the morning, and that kind of schedule hardly ever makes for a happy, healthy marriage.

I was only about eight years old, yet every night I slept with one eye open, waiting for the sound of the door unlocking, a signal that he was finally home. I'd catch just a glimpse of his silhouette climbing the darkened stairs, and then brace myself for the possibility of another argument between my parents.

Most nights, that argument came. There were rare moments of peace when I could fall asleep, but no matter what the circumstance, I'd wake up for school with a smile the next morning.

I never let family turmoil drag me down. I tucked it away and kept moving forward, determined to stay positive. I don't know where that inner strength came from, but even at a young age, I had tunnel vision on the kind of life I wanted.

I wasn't angry with my father. I just accepted that, because they were my parents, they were the best in their own way.

He was quiet, a mystery of a man who rarely offered fatherly advice, but that mystery only made the road I traveled more my own.

The way I looked at it, Sometimes, marriages simply don't work out. I've always lived by the K-I-S-S rule: Keep it simple, stupid.

Don't over complicate things.

The Day I Met My Father

After about six months, things shifted.

My father sold the bar/lounge business and returned to the plumber's union.

It was a hot summer day in Jackson Heights when my Uncle Rich showed up with my two cousins, Charlie and Louis.

Their visits were always a blast. Our house, much like later on in Corona, was right down the block from what we affectionately called The Park, a true home away from home.

I was about nine, playing card games for nickels, dimes, and quarters against older teenagers.

It was 1971, a time when sniffing glue was all the rage, and I'd watch these older kids get completely wasted right before my eyes.

It was wild, and I had front-row seats to it all. Besides cards, we loved basketball. On this fateful day, while hanging out at the local shopping center, we encountered four black kids our age with a basketball.

I struck up a conversation, and soon enough, we all agreed to head to The Park for a game. Each of them had a bike, so we hopped on and rode together.

It was a lazy afternoon. My father was off working his plumber's job in the city, while Uncle Rich and Diamond were relaxing on the porch outside our house.

We split up for the ride. My brother and Louis took the route down seventy-seventh, while Charlie and I rode along seventy-sixth, where our house stood. Innocently, my cousin and I waved to our uncle and Diamond as we passed by. Pure, unadulterated innocence.

But suddenly, it was as if we'd committed a heinous crime. My uncle yelled out for us to get off the bikes immediately. I was confused, a little embarrassed, and honestly, a bit angry.

We told our new friends to continue without us and made our way to the porch. There, my uncle was livid not because we were on bikes, but because we were hanging out with black kids. I was shocked and pissed.

I thought, *This has got to be a joke.* I was only nine, and even then I knew this was fucking insane. His punishment was swift and severe. We were forced to stay inside for the rest of that beautiful summer day, staring at the wall.

I even told him, "You're not my father. You can't punish me!"

His response? "Your father will be home in an hour, and we'll let him decide."

That day, I lost all respect for him. An asshole, plain and simple.

I couldn't help but worry: *How would my father react when he got home?*

At that time, he was something of a mystery to me. I was nervous, praying that his reaction would be different, that he'd make me proud.

And after what felt like an eternity, he finally arrived. My heart was pounding. I rushed to him and explained everything.

My father, initially puzzled, turned to me with an intensity that made it clear he wasn't about to tolerate prejudice. "Michael, go get your basketball and go out and play!" he commanded.

Then, pulling me aside, he added, "Don't ever listen to your uncle; he's an idiot."

At that moment, I felt like a million dollars. I was so proud that man was my father. That day, I truly met the real him—a moment more profound than any lengthy sermon or fatherly advice. It was a lesson in loyalty, in standing by your beliefs.

My father wasn't just loyal to the people he cared about; he was loyal to his own convictions. That lesson runs through my veins to this day.

I often wonder what might have been if he'd reacted like my uncle.

As children, we absorb lessons from our parents—good or bad.

Unbeknownst to me at the time, my father taught me to judge people by who they are, not by what they look like. And that is a lesson I'll carry with me forever.

Back at the Penitentiary

There was a knock on the open office door, a signal that someone was about to step in.

I turned to find an older gentleman introducing himself as Supervisor Doreste. A veteran of the federal system, he was the kind of man who had seen it all. Cordial yet businesslike, he embodied the classic "penitentiary script," no small talk, no bullshit—just here to do his job and move on.

He informed me that he was there to escort me to the final destination of this grim road trip, the prison morgue.

I rose and followed him out, noting that he offered no condolences or displays of emotion, nothing that would have felt anything but superficial.

As we walked, he casually mentioned that I was his fifth, and the last, identification of the day.

To the outside world, death in a prison system might seem like an anomaly, but in reality, people pass on every day—whether from age, violence, suicide, or health complications.

I got the sense that for Supervisor Doreste, overseeing inmate identifications was as routine as grabbing a cup of coffee.

I appreciated his silence. Any extra words would have felt contrived.

He had a job to do, and I wasn't expecting him to don a mask of false sympathy.

We headed for the elevator. With a single press of the down arrow, it was clear we were heading to the building's basement.

When the elevator doors slid open, we paused as a gurney—its body draped in a sheet—was wheeled out.

I assumed it was an inmate being prepared for burial. We stepped into the elevator, and Doreste pressed the button labeled MORGUE.

Two floors later, we arrived.

Expecting a dim, eerie atmosphere, I was instead met by bright fluorescent lights and the sterile vibe of a hospital corridor. I trailed behind him down a hallway marked MORGUE.

At our destination, he swiped his identification card at an electronic door. Slowly, it swung open to reveal about ten doors lining one wall, each a refrigerated tomb bearing a handwritten number.

Supervisor Doreste scanned a desk, running his fingers along a form until he found the number: **#07659-143.**

He then located the matching door, opened it, and pulled out a gurney. At that moment, a crushing realization hit me: My father was identified by a number.

The sight left me feeling defeated and dejected.

"Take your time," Doreste said quietly. "And when you're ready to leave, just let me know. I'll be sitting right outside the door."

End of the Road

When a loved one passes, regardless of your age, you suddenly become an adult. You're no longer just somebody's child.

It's a moment of reflection, a painful realization that a chapter in your life has closed. I recalled all the memories and unsaid words: Diamond, the road trips, the pizza places, the Garment Center, racetrack days, California, that time I hit a deer, Grandma Josie, and that day in Jackson Heights when I finally understood who my father was.

Truth be told, from the time I was eleven until now, my father was always there for my siblings and me.

He relished having us around, and we worked together in every business he ran. Even when the federal government intervened and time separated us, we always picked up where we left off when he returned home.

Sure, there was dysfunction. What family doesn't have its own issues?

In the old western movies, the good guys wore white hats and the bad guys wore black. My Mom taught us that there was a better way. She showed us to wear the white hat, while my father, you can say, wore the black.

Today, we all sport white hats. Though mine might have a black band, if you catch my drift.

I understand that life is short, and we can't live in yesterday's shadow, but I'll keep those memories close to my heart for a lifetime.

Oh, and by the way—my father's name was **ANTHONY CONTE**, and he just wasn't fucking #07659-143.

13

One Helluva Ride

As I sat in that room alone with my father's lifeless body, an overwhelming emptiness took hold—my soul's voice completely silenced.

I was numb.

When you suffer an unexpected loss, life has a way of humbling you, stripping away pretenses, and exposing your vulnerabilities and insecurities.

In that moment, the thought *I could have been better* clawed at my spirit. Each of us rides our own personal roller coaster, the wild, unpredictable journey of life, often forgetting the importance of those we truly depend on.

When things go awry, there are a few special people you can count on without fail. And yet, we sometimes take them for granted, stashing them away for a rainy day with excuses like, "I've been swamped at work," "The kids are sick," or "My weekends are crazy." We chase after new, shiny distractions, prioritizing today while relegating yesterday to the rear-view mirror.

It's sad how life can pull us away from those who love us unconditionally, even if it's never intentional.

I will leave you with this. It's a fast-moving roller coaster and we're all just trying to get our money's worth.

You know exactly what I mean.

Hope

I slowly pushed the gurney back into its refrigerated tomb and gently closed the numbered door. I stared at that cold number—#07659-143—for a long ten seconds before turning away.

In that moment, all my defiance melted away; I was simply broken.

I leaned on my faith and, as always, found the answer I needed.

Reading this book, you might think my favorite four-letter word starts with an F.

Sure, I've used it often, but my true favorite is H-O-P-E. Hope!

So the answer I found was hope.

That the hope for tomorrow will bring acceptance and offer me strength to carry on my journey, a beacon of understanding and positivity that I've clung to my entire life.

It's the promise of better days ahead, the very thing I hang my hat on. Hope is my equivalent of saying "YES"—a positive, unwavering force.

The Point of No Return

I left the morgue, and just as promised, Supervisor Doreste was waiting for me on the other side of the door.

He was calmly sipping a cup of coffee, exuding the respectful, no-nonsense demeanor of a man who's done this a hundred times.

He gave me all the time I needed for my final prison visit.

When I finally told him, "I'm ready," he tossed his coffee in the trash, and we retraced our steps back to the elevator. Back to the same corridor, the same elevator that brought me back to the main floor where I earlier met with Administrator Milo.

Doreste informed me that my next task was to receive my father's death certificate. He directed me to yet another office—one that, like all government offices, exuded drab colors and featured an American flag standing proudly in the corner.

There, an older gentleman named Officer Mosca greeted me with a firm handshake and a polite manner. He asked for my identification; I handed over my driver's license without hesitation.

When he inquired how many certificates I needed, I stammered, "I...I...I guess five should be sufficient."

Without missing a beat, Officer Mosca walked over to a large metal file cabinet, retrieved a printer, and soon printed five copies.

He placed them in a large white envelope, on which he had simply written CONTE. No number in sight.

Surprised, I met his gaze as he offered a handshake and a knowing wink.

In a quiet tone, he said, "I knew your dad. He was a good man. Sorry for your loss. Good luck."

We shared an understanding at that moment. I shook his hand firmly, filled with gratitude, and then walked out of his office.

Good Riddance

I headed back down the same long corridor Officer Bruckner once pointed out, a corridor that seemed to stretch on forever.

In the distance, I could just make out the reception desk and the doors to the outside world. I quickly texted my brother.

Hey Dave. Leaving this miserable place. Be at the car in 5.

His reply came swiftly.

All good, I'm here with Cousin.

Eager to escape that hellhole, I picked up my pace.

At the reception area, I caught Officer Bruckner's eye, waved a quick thanks his way, and stepped out.

I spotted my SUV immediately and made a beeline for it.

The rain was coming down hard on this unusually warm early June evening.

As I walked in the pouring rain, a numbness still clung to me. Numb from my father's sudden, cold departure from this world, and yet, a sense of relief began to wash over me. I realized I'd never have to return to that place again.

I didn't even rush; I let the warm rain soak into me, a cleansing that, strangely, offered comfort.

Finally reaching the car, I hopped into the back seat where Dave was driving and my cousin sat in the passenger seat.

I didn't hesitate. "Let's get the fuck outta here."

Leaving, But Not Letting Go

Driving out of Lewisburg, guilt gnawed at me for leaving my father's body behind. I understood we couldn't take him with us, but abandoning him in that cold, institutional place felt wrong.

I wrestled with those feelings. As we passed the entrance, I glanced back at the Lewisburg sign and, just like when we arrived, noticed the towering one-hundred-foot guard tower.

Silence reigned in the car until I finally broke it. "You know what I realized?" I said slowly. "Our differences can be our strengths."

Dave glanced at me through the rear-view mirror. "What do you mean?"

I replied, "Our unique approaches to life earned us a deep, mutual respect for our father. We knew his way wasn't for us. But embracing our differences forged a powerful love and loyalty that held our family together."

"Here's a man whose very existence gave us a life that few could ever dream of. Sure, his life brought chaos, anxiety, and fear. Abso-fucking-lutely! But on the flip side, you, me, and Grace would've taken a bullet for that guy, wouldn't we?"

I continued, "Maybe our shared experiences with him not only helped us understand who he was but also propelled our own personal growth. There was acceptance, not rejection. Maybe we aren't that different after all."

Dave's eyes filled with tears, and he simply whispered, "Amen."

One Helluva Ride

That day marked the end of one helluva ride—a ride full of pain, memories, and hard truths.

It was a ride that forced me to grow up overnight, to face loss, and to discover that sometimes, hope is all you have to keep moving forward.

And even though the road ahead would be forever altered by grief and reflection, I knew that I'd carry my father's story, and the lessons it taught me, with pride, all the way down the road.

It's Time to Go

We drove in silence for about forty-five minutes because, really, what's there to say at that moment?

Next to me sat a white envelope filled with death certificates.

I never bothered asking anyone at Lewisburg about the cause of death; why inquire of someone who likely didn't give a damn?

So, I unfastened the clasp and pulled out the certificate. The first detail that caught my eye was the Time of Death: 3:09 a.m.

My gaze then jumped to the Cause of Death. Natural causes.

I murmured, "Dave, Cuz, it was natural causes."

Dave replied, "Thank God it wasn't a heart attack with him struggling. I figured he was quietly summoned, like a silent command to pack his bags. It's time to go."

"True," I agreed and made the sign of the cross.

Then, out of respect, my cousin asked, "How old was he?"

Both Dave and I replied in unison, "86." I added, "Diamond was 91 when he passed. They both had a good run."

Three Hungry Men

After another fifteen minutes on the road, my cousin suddenly piped up, "You guys hungry?"

I immediately shot back, "Starving!"

Dave chimed in, "Let's eat!"

I glanced at the dashboard clock, 6:26 p.m., and realized I hadn't eaten for hours. Mentally exhausted and physically feeling washed out, I needed food.

We soon spotted a sign featuring various symbols: a gas station, choices for fast food, and, notably, a sign that simply read DINER.

It was an easy choice. Old reliable, the diner. We decided to kill two birds with one stone and fill up the tank first, then grab some dinner.

Driving on Route 80, our GPS showed 133 miles to Queens, but Dave took the next exit marked 224 I-80E, DANVILLE. We followed the signs without fuss.

At the gas station, my cousin yelled, "I got it!" He leapt out, filled up the tank, and paid.

Dave and I started to protest, "Whoa, what are you doing? Let us help you..." but Cousin quickly shot back, "Shut the fuck up, no worries."

We didn't want to take away his blessing, so we simply thanked him. That's what family—and good friends—do.

We then headed to the diner, about a mile to the south. The parking lot had only three cars, and it was a slow, quiet night—the perfect setting for what we needed: peace, quiet, and a good meal.

We parked, stepped inside, and asked for a table in the corner where we could sit undisturbed.

A friendly young lady named Irene greeted us, taking our beverage order with an infectious smile. She radiated good vibes and genuine goodwill; you could tell she was one of the good ones.

Hungry as we were, we quickly placed our food order. "Slow night," she remarked, "your food should be out right away."

That was music to our ears.

A Different Kind of Story

Once our beers arrived, Dave raised a toast to my father.

We clinked glasses and quietly began to reminisce, not dwelling on the present loss but celebrating the qualities that made my father who he was.

You know, you can drive down different roads and follow various paths, but what's under the hood can still be perfectly aligned.

My cousin broke in, "You know what I'll always remember about your dad? He was always courteous and polite with everyone, a true gentleman with a capital G. He always pulled for the underdog; that quality endeared him to so many."

Dave nodded in agreement saying, "Well said. No doubt."

In a low, deliberate tone, I added, "Cousin, let me tell you a quick story that ties right into that. When he ran his business, Classic Fit, we encountered all kinds of characters, powerful, smart, intimidating, hilarious, and sometimes downright treacherous."

"But my father once met a young black kid—must've been nineteen or twenty—scrambling for work. This poor kid, with an awful stutter and a slight mental disability, could barely say his own name. Calvin."

"Only God knows how much that kid suffered from bullying and abuse. I can't recall exactly how they met—maybe he was looking for work at a restaurant, cleaning offices, or running errands—but my father saw something in him. He befriended Calvin and immediately gave him a job at Classic Fit. Dave, you remember him, right?"

"Of course, he was with us five days a week," Dave replied.

I continued, "My father had Calvin delivering fine fabrics, buttons, and other items to vendors. In time, he even trusted Calvin with bank deposits. He paid him a weekly salary, a nice piece of change. That trust gave Calvin purpose and self-respect. I watched in awe as Calvin transformed; his confidence grew, and his communication skills improved dramatically. The world changes when someone believes in you. I gotta tell you, Cousin, it was a blessing to witness. My father wasn't doing it for accolades; he simply did what was right. He even bought him lunch every day and made sure no one messed with him."

"Once word got out that 'he was with us,' Calvin became untouchable. Most people wouldn't bother. It's either 'Who cares?' or 'Who's got the time?' But my father, with all his toughness, had a goodness that left a profound impact on me. It taught me to always lend a hand to the fallen and the misfortunate. I don't have to give back. I want to give back! It's not hard to be courteous and caring. It's not just what I preach; it's what I live by. Cousin, I learned that from my father. It's made me a better husband, father, and man, and a lesson I pass on to my children, hoping it echoes through generations."

Just then, Irene reappeared with a tray of food. With a bright smile, she said, "Buon Appetite."

We attacked our meal like it was our last supper.

After we finished, we asked for the check. Irene handed it to me with a warm smile and a friendly goodbye. Once again, my cousin insisted on paying, I knew it was with love and respect for my father.

I ended up settling the bill, and as we left, we waved farewell to Irene. Outside, we encountered an older gentleman, the owner, and, in the spirit of my father, we took a moment to tell him how special Irene was and how satisfied we were with our dining experience.

It was our way of paying it forward. I'm sure my father would have approved. There's a saying, "Don't judge a book by its cover," something I'd have inscribed on his tombstone.

We left the diner and continued the last leg of our road trip, carrying our memories, our grief, and a promise to always pay forward the love we received.

If someone asked me, "Is this the hill you want to die on?"

My answer is a simple Yes.

The End of The Road Trip

As we headed for the car, Cousin insisted he'd drive the rest of this helluva ride. I was beyond exhausted, a blessing in disguise.

"Cousin, appreciate you. I'm off my feet; it's been a long day," I said.

Dave handed him the key to my SUV, and with genuine relief in his voice, he added, "Thank you, my cousin."

I jumped into the back seat while Dave took shotgun. We were all eager to get back to Queens. The clock read 8:06, and our GPS ETA was 10:13.

At that moment, I felt like that kid again—forty years ago in Danny's 1983 Aries K, limping home in a demolished car after hitting a deer. I couldn't wait to see the sign that read NEW YORK. No disrespect to Pennsylvania, but I was sick of this fucking state.

I texted Toni to let her know I was on my way and what time to expect me. Then I messaged Grace, promising to call her in the morning to discuss the details, and I asked how our mother was doing. To pass the time, Cousin started rambling about his sister, Tina, and her divorce from Peter, dating in 1980, marrying in 1985, and now divorced in 2023.

"I don't understand. Married thirty-eight fucking years, three kids, grandkids, and *now* you get a divorce? Where the fuck is she going? Tell me, cousins, does that make any sense?" he ranted.

I didn't really know what to say. What can you say about someone else's business? With all the sadness of the past six hours weighing on us, I decided a little joke might lighten the mood. "Cousin, I guess Peter never 'put Tina in the seat of a Cadillac Biarritz...'"

(If you recall earlier in the story, she demanded that at the wedding reception—a tug of war for being a 'well-kept wife').

We all burst into laughter as we headed back toward New York.

Within fifteen minutes, I dozed off and didn't wake until we were back in Corona. We pulled into my brother's driveway, and Cousin made his way to his car. I hugged them both, then got behind the wheel and drove to my house on Long Island. It was a long day to say the least.

The Winners Circle, Part 2

The next morning, June 5, I was jolted awake by my phone ringing.

One ring...two rings...three rings...I grabbed it, glancing at my nightstand clock: 9:15 a.m. Rubbing my eyes, I answered on the third ring.

"Hello, Mr. Conte? Supervisor Doreste, Lewisburg Penitentiary."

At first, I was annoyed. So fucking early! But I kept my composure and replied politely, "Yes, hello, Supervisor."

Doreste quickly continued, "Just reaching out to confirm the name and address of the funeral home you'd like your father's body transported to."

I got hit with a lightning bolt. Holy fuck, this isn't a dream. This really happened!

I quickly responded, "Carneys Funeral Home," and provided the address in Corona.

He thanked me and informed me that my father's body would leave the facility by 11 a.m. and should arrive at the funeral home by 4. I thanked him, hung up, and then called Carneys to relay the details. I also reached out to Grace and Dave.

Navigating the preparations for the deceased is a surreal, robotic experience. You simply follow the road-map of requirements, emotionlessly pushing forward. Do you really have a choice? After coordinating with Grace and Dave, we set the wake service June 9 and funeral for June 10.

The wake was everything we expected: flowers everywhere, people from all walks of life pouring into the funeral home, a perfect representation of the lives our family had lived. There were doctors, lawyers, financial professionals, construction workers, beauticians, and, of course, my father's "friends."

It was a snapshot of the balancing act that defined our family life.

My siblings and I stood by the coffin, greeting people as they approached. A family member mentioned there was a line down the block waiting to get in—mostly men, his old friends, who couldn't have been more complimentary and caring.

Absolute gentlemen! The most common comments were, "I loved your father. He was like a second father to me," and "I can't begin to tell you what that man did for me," and "A man's man. They don't make them like him anymore."

Over and over, the heartfelt and honest emotion poured in. It filled me with pride and cemented how deeply he was respected as a man.

It got me thinking. I was dead wrong when I used to say he always ended up in "second place." In his world, he was clearly in the winners circle, though I might have been too blind to see it at times. I was viewing life with a different set of lenses.

We all live in our small corners of this universe; if you're revered and respected in your corner, that's all that matters.

Am I right?

Fuck the opinions of others. In the end, you win.

Two Months Later

It was a hot summer day, ninety-one degrees out, but add New York's signature humidity, and it felt like a hundred and five.

Days like that are why they invented air conditioning; you could literally fry an egg on the sidewalk. And, as fate would have it, it was also my son's birthday, August 6.

We were celebrating in the backyard by the pool while I was getting ready to fire up the barbecue. I climbed out of the pool and headed inside to prep the burgers, ribs, and chicken.

As I walked into the kitchen, I noticed a small stack of mail on the table. I shuffled through the envelopes: credit card bills, electric and phone bills, and three envelopes of junk. Then, the last piece of mail caught my eye. It was addressed to me.

I recognized the handwriting immediately. It was my father's.

What the fuck! I thought. In the upper left-hand corner, the return address read:
Anthony Conte   #07659-143
United States Penitentiary, Lewisburg

I was in shock. Why on earth was I receiving a letter from my father two months after his death? How?

I grabbed the letter and rushed to my home office to read it. My hands shook so badly, I could feel the air leaving my lungs. I took a deep breath, closed my eyes, exhaled, and then opened it.

The letter was dated June 2, 2023, just the day before he died. It read:

Dear Michael,

Hey, long time no see. Hoping all is well with you, Toni, and the kids.

How's my great-grandson? Looking at the pictures you sent, he seems like an amazing little guy. Give everyone a hug for me.

My days are just like any other. One turns into the next. It can wear you down at times, but you get used to it, I guess.

I've been playing cards with my friends, though sometimes that gets a little crazy, so I take breaks from all the bullshit to go for walks in the yard. I can't move like I used to, so my walks are about 20 minutes at a brisk clip.

I spend many nights in my bunk reading or listening to music. Sinatra, Bennett, you know the classics. It takes me back to the old days. My father, my mother, my brother, and your mother when we were dating. How is she? I know she's been sick and not doing too well. Send her my regards.

I made many mistakes in my day, and when you're sitting in this fucking hole, all you do is think of how I could have done better. Too late now. All I have is regret that taps me on the shoulder and wakes me up every morning. I wanted to reach out and tell you how proud I am of the man you've become, a husband, a father, now a grandfather.

You've done well. It's crazy, but I never told you those words all these years. I guess it's easier for me to let my emotions out when I have a pen in my hand. I wish I'd said this in person, face to face. That's on me. I'm

86. Can you believe it? Jeez, I feel like I'm on borrowed time. Who the fuck knows? It could be any minute, day, or week.

Now, as an old man nearing the end, I realize things today that I wish I'd known fifty years ago. What I lost and what I sacrificed for my own selfish needs. I see now that the roads I should have taken might have given you, Dave, and Grace an easier path.

I hope you forgive me. I'm truly sorry, and I want you to know I always loved you. Now that you're a man, I hold you in the highest regard.

Let's not kid ourselves, I may be dead soon. I'm using this moment as a cleansing. I want you to understand that my intentions were always good. I thought my actions and choices were best for the family.

Now, with death at my doorstep and all my fear and embarrassment gone, I can honestly say I did wrong, and I'm sorry from the bottom of my heart. Hope I can make it up to you on the other side...

Take Care, Kid
Love, Dad

I must have read that letter five times, maybe more. I went over every word, every sentence, with tears welling up in my eyes. I felt, just as he did, that I should have said more when he was alive.

I wish I'd expressed how much he meant to me. It's a fault of most men—silence. "Oh, they know how I feel." "I can't say that!" "Real men are stoic!" "I'm not a fucking pussy!"

Always the worst mistake a man can make is not speaking his truth. I raise my hand and accept my fault. We all finally realize our foolish ways when we hit a crossroad, be it sickness, heartbreak, or like my father, staring death in the face.

After reading his letter, I understood that my father was letting his cuts bleed so, in turn, I could make mine heal. It opened my eyes to change.

Today I even talk about that change with my siblings who received similar letters from our dad. How his life and words shaped us, how they helped us show more emotion, talk openly with others, and be honest with each other. He taught us to speak our truth.

See Where the River Takes Us

I began this story with Robert Frost's poem, *The Road Not Taken*, a piece often hailed as an anthem for individualism. Frost himself admitted it was a "tricky poem," noting that the two roads in the wood could be interchangeable, equally traveled. Given our circumstances, who really knows what the right choice is?

The answer reveals itself only at the end of one's journey. The poem leaves us to wonder: Do our choices lead to contentment or regret? I'll leave that for you to decide.

As for my father, I feel his path was marked by regret. But then again, that's just my perspective, viewpoints can vary widely.

Isn't that what makes the world go 'round?

Sometimes, the simplest approach is best: Just see where the river takes us.

K-I-S-S—Keep It Simple, Stupid.

You might wonder if I came out of all this damaged? Well, I would first say it depends on who you ask. No seriously, I would absolutely say, No. There are many others who unfortunately have gone through a lot worse.

However, my experience only deepened my empathy and understanding for those fighting their own struggles. I stand with the underdog because I've been there, done that.

In that scorching summer heat, amid birthday celebrations and poolside barbecues, my father's letter—unexpected, haunting, and full of raw honesty—brought everything crashing back. It forced me to confront my own regrets, my silence, and the choices I made. It reminded me to keep moving, to let the river of life carry me forward, and to never forget where I came from, even when the road gets rough.

It's said we only get one shot at life, and if that's the gospel you have tucked under your arm, then for what it's worth, it's been One Helluva Ride...

Final Thoughts

As I neared the end of this book, I wrote these words with a broken heart. My mother, my rock, passed away after a long, brutal battle with leukemia and dementia. When she was diagnosed, they gave her a year to live. Her doctor had no idea who he was dealing with!

True to form, she fought on and lived another eight years. My mom was the essence of my soul, the very core of who I am and what I represent. All her practical teachings and hard-won advice flowed into me, and I count myself lucky every single day.

Though her physical presence is gone, her spirit and energy live on in my brother, sister, and me. Even as she slowly deteriorated, she taught us to face a terrible disease with courage, dignity, and an unwavering respect for others.

She fought all her life, steadfast in her beliefs and convictions, an independent thinker from whom I learned at the feet of a master. Her integrity and kindness inspired countless people. She always preached that the people who matter aren't judged by the size of their bank account or the car they drive, they're measured by their integrity, honesty, and straightforwardness.

I remember as a kid, she'd ask, "Michael, how much homework did your teacher give you today?" I'd reply, "Oh, I don't know, Ma, it was a lot."

And then she'd hit me with the lesson I'd carry forever. "Michael, A LOT IS WHERE YOU PARK YOUR CAR. BE MORE SPECIFIC!" It hit me like a ton of bricks. For those first few seconds, I didn't know how to respond until I realized she expected a clear, direct answer.

That lesson—to be straightforward and honest—became a mantra in my everyday life.

My mom fought for the souls of my siblings and me. Surrounded by a force that could have overwhelmed anyone, she wasn't trying to change people's approach to life; she was adamant about how she wanted her children's lives to evolve.

Every family has its own history, a family tree with roots that stretch back through generations. And sometimes, one person changes everything and creates a new branch that benefits every future generation. My mother was that person in our family.

I've always been fascinated by the lives and struggles of my ancestors. I wish their voices could speak to me today. You might wonder, why write this story? I'm no celebrity, so who would be interested? The truth is, I wrote this book for my entire family—my wife, children, grandchildren, brother, sister, nieces, and nephews.

I wanted to give them a glimpse of what came before, to preserve our family's legacy. Most importantly, I wanted to leave behind my mother's voice, the sound of her strength, her wisdom, courage and the impact she had on us all.

Ma, I love you and miss you. On behalf of your entire family, thank you. We will continue to make you proud.

Thank you for being my voice of reason and for saving my life.

Bedtime at 11 p.m.... talk tonight.

Love,
Michael

Michael Conte

Michael Conte resides on Long Island, New York, with his wife. He is forever grateful for the unwavering support of his wife and his adult children who continue to be his inspiration. He is a blessed grandfather. Michael enjoys spending a great deal of time at his winter home in Florida with family and friends. He believes that your best days are waiting for you, and the "underdog" position in life is only temporary.

www.ingramcontent.com/pod-product-compliance
Lightning Source LLC
Chambersburg PA
CBHW021422110726
47901CB00008B/2269